VAMPIRES
OF THE
CROSS

and other musings

DR. LARRY KINCHELOE

ISBN: 978-1-09835-173-1 (print)

ISBN: 978-1-09835-174-8 (eBook)

VAMPIRES OF THE CROSS
and other musings

VAMPIRES OF THE CROSS.....1

CONSTRUCTS.....15

COOKING TROLL.....20

EYE OF THE BEHOLDER.....23

GIGGLY GOOD.....30

GROUPON 2050.....33

GYNO TO THE STARS.....37

HOW SMALL.....42

HOWLING AT THE MOON.....45

NEVER TRUST A TROLL.....50

NINE SILLY ELECTRONS.....55

NUMBERS.....59

PRAYERS TO THE GALACTIC GOD.....67

QUARANTINE.....69

LIFE SAVER.....76

SMALL SAVIOR.....80

TAU CETI.....88

TEXT FROM GOD.....100

THE CLOUD.....119

THE DARK.....130

THE DEVIL'S DELIVERY.....136

THE IT GUY.....142

THE DRAIN.....148

THE LAST SHALL BE FIRST.....159

THE POST CARD.....170

TIME BUBBLE.....175

TRUE BELIEVER.....185

OCCAM'S RAZOR.....189

ODE TO THE HUNT.....212

VAMPIRES OF THE CROSS

THE STARK LIGHT OF FLUORESCENT BULBS BATHED THE ROOM in a harsh, cold luminosity. In the center of the room a metal chair was fastened to the floor with bolts. In the chair sat a man. Straps of thick, leather dug into the skin of his chest and thighs, securing him in place. His wrists and legs were bound with metal clamps. The shine on the straps indicated that this prison chair had never before been used. A nondescript wooden table and chair was the only other furniture. His head hung forward and it was hard to tell if he was asleep or dead.

The stillness of the cement block room was shattered by the metallic echoes which heralded the unbolting of a large door - the only entrance or exit. The door creaked open as the metal hinges struggled against their weighty load. A priest walked into the room carrying a short, two-handed sword. He moved the chair so he was facing the captive. The priest held the sword in his lap and for several moments he observed the man strapped to the chair. The priest noted that the man had dark skin and facial features indicating Mediterranean heritage. His mind struggled with the concept that even though the man looked to be in his late thirties, he was actually over two thousand years old.

"So, you are the last," the priest spoke.

There was no reaction for several moments and then the captive slowly raised his head to look at the cleric. The man stared at the priest with piercing brown, almost black eyes.

"So, Priest, which future is it going to be?" he asked in a deep, gravelly voice.

After a reflective pause, he released a weary sigh. "I don't know. I never really thought this day would come. For hundreds of years, we have been searching for you and have killed many of your children to make this day a reality."

"They are not my children," spat out the man with obvious disgust. "They were a mistake born out of ignorance and loneliness."

"Well, Anthony-"

"Antonius," the man interrupted. "I would like to be called by my given Roman name since this may be the last time I will ever hear it."

"Fair enough, Antonius, fair enough," agreed the priest. Out of habit he smoothed out the creases of his ecclesiastic robe.

He did not look like a priest, Antonius thought. His eyes were the color blue that he had seen in the waters of the Caribbean. The skin was dark and weathered but he carried himself as a man with great strength.

They stared at each other for several moments in heavy silence until the priest began to think that they were in an unspoken contest of wills.

Then the bound man broke the silence. "You want to know what really happened, don't you? You want to know the truth."

"Yes," replied the priest. "Much of what we know has been passed down by myths and legends and has been corrupted over the millennia depending on which of the conflicted church factions were in power at the time."

"Well, I guess it's time to set the record straight. To clear up all the lies that have been propagated by your church over the past two thousand years."

From a pocket in his robes, the priest produced an iPhone and opened the recording application before placing the device on the table. "I am ready," he said as he hit the red button.

The prisoner began to speak. "There were five of us in the beginning. Hannah, Isaiah, Ruben, David and myself."

"How were you transformed into what you are today?" asked the priest.

"There were three men. Misguided zealots who believed the literal words of the teacher when he said that drinking his blood would give them eternal life."

The priest quickly scanned his memory of the Bible and found the teachings in the sixth Chapter of John, verse 53. He frowned at the implications of the statement.

"After the teacher's body was taken away, they scraped the dried blood from the cross and at some point, drank a mixture of blood and wine."

"And the girl, Hannah?" prompted the priest.

"She, like me, was an unfortunate accident. She was part of the group of women who were preparing the body for burial. When removing the wreath of thorns from his head, she was stuck with one of the bloody thorns."

"And you?"

"My story is found in John 19:34." He paused and waited to see how long it would take the priest to make the connection.

A look of surprise crossed his face. "So, *you* were the soldier, the soldier who pierced his side with a spear."

"At the time, I saw him as just another convicted prisoner and I was just doing my job," Antonius said with a shrug. "As I cleaned off the tip of my spear, I cut myself which was my ticket to the little drama we now play out." He paused, "May I have something to drink?"

The priest pondered the request, rose from his chair and walked to the heavy metal door. The door creaked as it opened. This led the prisoner to believe that they must be under a watchful eye – perhaps a hidden surveillance camera. The priest spoke briefly to an unseen person, waited a few moments and then returned with a bottle of water.

He walked back to the prisoner and gently held the bottle out so he could drink. The act felt to the priest as if he were giving communion to one of the faithful or performing last rites.

After several gulps, the prisoner said, "Thank you. I think I can go on now."

He paused as if trying to collect his thoughts. "The three zealots, Isaiah, Ruben, and David, lived their lives with the expectation that something would be different. For Hannah and myself, we were unaware of what happened to us and it took years to finally understand. I found myself healthier and stronger even though I was almost forty years old which was past my prime as a Roman centurion."

Antonius tentatively tested his metal shackles.

"Titanium?"

"No, this is a new product which combines graphene and maraging steel."

"Ah, all very high tech."

"We didn't want to take any chances."

"I understand. Well, about a year later, our unit was ordered to the northeast quadrant of Gaul to put down an uprising of the Germanic tribes. I was wounded many times but I seemed to have developed the unusual ability to heal quickly. But when I survived a battle axe to the back, the other soldiers began to treat me differently and I heard murmurings about me being cursed or blessed, depending on the person. I was moved from unit to unit as my story made company commander's uncomfortable. I still had not made the connection between my new abilities and the blood of the prophet."

"Your fellow soldiers must have been afraid of you," summized the priest.

"Yes, but I stayed in the legion because it was the only life I knew. But then during the battle of Medway in Britain I used the confusion to slip away from the battle and spent the next many years roaming the Highlands. I should have been an old man in my seventies but by now it was obvious that I was no longer aging."

"When did you finally understand what had happened?"

"I was married twice but the pain of watching women I loved grow old and die while I remained unchanged was just too much. So, after two hundred years, I decided to return to Jerusalem where this all began. The early Christian church was in turmoil at this time. The three zealots had remained part of the early church and their story was known to the inner circle of priests. After the death of the prophet, his followers had expected him to return during their lifetime and when it became obvious that this was not going to happen, the inner circle of the church started looking for answers. Are you familiar with the twenty-first chapter of Luke where it says 'Truly I tell you; this generation will certainly not pass away until all these things have happened'?"

"Yes," the priest said in a hushed tone as the implications coalesced in his own mind.

"Well, the hierarchy of the church was in conflict about what to do with the three men. Some felt they should be killed so the last of "that generation" would pass away to set the stage for the return of the prophet. Others felt that since everything was under the control of God, this must be the way events were supposed to play out. Isaiah, Ruben, and David became fearful for their lives and left Jerusalem, trying to escape into obscurity. But the church could never agree on how to handle the situation and so two factions developed." He paused and then asked, "Which following do you owe allegiance to?"

"I don't understand," the priest replied.

"Well, if you are member of *Coelus Nova* then you are here to kill me because you believe this will usher in a new Heaven and Earth. If you are here to protect me then I would assume that you are a member of the order of *Veritas Deus* who believes that God is in control and man should not alter the normal course of events. I also sometimes suspect that members of Veritas Deus are somewhat afraid of what this new heaven and earth would look like and are quite happy to have things stay the same."

"I follow neither of those orders," interjected the priest. His tone was that of icy metal.

"Oh," replied Antonius. "Then you must be here because of," he paused, "*revenge.*" The last word was said with a hiss.

"Yes, revenge. Some of your followers almost wiped out my family. One of your creations went rogue and massacred the small farming town of Belmont, Kansas in 1877. Only three small children, who had been hidden in a root cellar, survived. My great grandfather was one of those children. This was six months after the seventh Calvary massacre at the Little Bighorn and so when 137 bodies were found with their throats ripped out, it was blamed on the Cheyenne and Arapahoe tribes. The children were placed in a Catholic orphanage and two priests were sent to investigate the unusual deaths. After viewing the carnage, they knew it was the work of a vampire but allowed the blame to fall on the natives. I grew up hearing impossible stories about vampires. I felt called to join the church. Partly out of conviction, but also as a way to find the truth. By the time I had worked myself into the Churches hierarchy, the other four prime vampires had already died or been killed. You are the last one."

"I am not... *we* were not vampires," spat out Antonius angrily. "You really don't know what happened, do you?"

"That is why I'm here. I am here to understand and to record. This may be your and our last chance to understand what really happened – what the truth really is."

There was a long pause and then Antonius let escape a long sigh. "The three zealots were known by the church but Hannah and myself were not discovered for hundreds of years. Hannah, like myself, survived by always keeping on the move. She first thought she could have a normal life. She got married, had children but when it was obvious that she was not aging, members of her village assumed that she must be a witch or at least possessed by a demon. Her husband begged her to leave for her own protection. I did hear that she snuck back into the village to attend funerals of her children when they died of old age. May I have some more water, please?"

The priest nodded and once again gave the prisoner his request.

"Eventually, loneliness drove us all to find someone with whom to share the decades. We were desperate to find companionship and love. Living forever is not all that it is cracked up to be. All of us thought that if blood of the prophet could keep us alive, then maybe our blood would keep our friends and loved ones alive as well. Sadly, we discovered that we were… horribly wrong in our assumptions. Those that drank our blood became the creatures which you know as vampires. Once again, the five of us were punished as we were forced to watch people we loved – our dearest friends become these abominations of nature…. *vampires.*"

"So, you had no idea," the priest started.

"Of course not. What sane person would want to turn someone into a creature that depends on the blood of innocents to survive? Once it became clear what was happening, everyone stopped the experiment of trying to convert a friend or loved one into an eternal partner. Unfortunately, our creations did not have the same belief and were more than willing to convert others to their status. Thus, started the myth and the reality of vampires and vampire hunters. The church has been very successful in elimination of these abominations."

The priest suddenly felt very old and very tired. He was developing a dull ache behind his eyes which he tried to rub from existence. The story of Antonius, if true, was nothing like what he had been led to believe by the church elders. For over two thousand years the story had been twisted. Parts had been lost, speculation had been added and none of the ancient texts accurately told the story that he was hearing today.

"I know it must be hard for you to believe everything you've been taught about this situation has been false."

The priest lifted his head and tilted his neck to the right and the left trying to stretch out the tension in his muscles with audible crackles and pops from his vertebrae.

"How did you become the last?" he asked after a moment.

"Ruben was the first to die. He was tracked down by members of the *Coelus Nova* and beheaded. His body was then hacked into many small pieces and then those pieces were sent to the four corners of the known world where they were burned and the ashes scattered to the sea. Overkill if you ask me." Antonius flashed a small smile at his play on words.

"You see, although we had great powers of regeneration and healing, we were not immortal. If our bodies are destroyed by fire, explosion, or decapitation, we die like any other living being."

Antonius looked at the short sword that the priest was holding.

"I see that you are holding a Japanese katana. My guess is that it is the real deal, not a replication."

"You know your blades."

"A soldier picks up a lot of information in two thousand years."

"Who was the next to die?" prodded the priest.

"After the death of Ruben, the others, Isaiah and David, were removed by members of the *Veritas Deus* to a secured monastery fortress in the village of Labro which is located on Mount Terminillo in central Italy."

"I have been there."

Antonius looked surprised. "You have?"

"Yes, when I was a seminary student, I once spent a summer in Italy visiting old monasteries. If I remember correctly, the monastery at Labro was destroyed by an earthquake."

"Earthquake," sneered Antonius, "it is amazing how many lies have been propagated by those who voice a belief in truth."

The priest said nothing.

"When Pope Leo X assumed power in 1521, he not only excommunicated Martin Luther and extended the Spanish inquisition into Portugal but he was a member of the *Coelus Nova* and he vowed that he would track down and destroy the remaining two members of the 'Last Generation' as they were called. He was the first Pope to go after these men with the full power and resources of the Vatican. Dozens of priests loyal to *Veritas Deus* were tortured until they gave up the location of the last two zealots. Don't you find it ironic how much death and destruction has been done by those who claim to follow the Prince of Peace?"

Antonius did not wait for an answer.

"The Vatican guard and a large mercenary force surrounded the monastery. They then pounded the monastery with mortar and cannon until no recognizable building was left standing. They dug through the rubble until they found the bodies of Isaiah and David. Their bodies were then tied to a keg of black powder and exploded. The members of the *Coelus Nova* then sat back and waited for the second coming, which never came. At this point there was much disillusionment among the church leaders as it became obvious over the decades that followed, that there was no ushering in of a new world and certainly there was no new Heaven on Earth.

"None of this is in the recorded histories," interjected the priest.

"Not in any of the histories that you have been allowed to read," corrected Antonius. He then continued, "The church then believed that if they eradicated all of the created abominations, that this would allow for the new order to arrive. They became very efficient at sending out groups of dedicated priests to eradicate all known vampires. I think the last known vampire was killed shortly after the death of your family. And then, once again, the church leaders waited expectantly for the new world order, but alas they were disappointed as still nothing changed. The orders of *Coelus Nova* and *Veritas Deus* then became relics of the past and faded away over the next one hundred years. The church had no knowledge of the existence of Hannah or myself, although every so often, rumors would pop up of an ageless man or woman and this would be our sign that it was time to move on."

"Did you ever meet her? Hannah?" asked the priest.

There was a long pause and the priest thought he saw a hint of sadness around the eyes of Antonius. Antonius cleared his throat and shifted as if he were trying to find a more comfortable spot within his shackles.

"It was 1922 and I was living in Chicago at the time. I had moved there shortly after the great fire in '71 to buy land at bargain prices for resale at a later date. Wealth is easy to obtain when time is on your side. I am not sure how she found me but she had also amassed enough financial resources to hire a small army of Pinkerton detectives."

"Did they try to capture you?" asked the priest.

"No, they just delivered a message and a train ticket to New York City with a boarding pass for the luxury liner *Majestic* headed to Liverpool."

"What was in…?"

"The message?" Antonius completed the priest's question. "The note read, 'I am like you and I need your help. Hannah.' In a life filled with the boredom of the ages, the invitation was too intriguing to ignore. So, I packed a bag and boarded the *Majestic*. There I found myself in adjoining first class cabins with a young woman who looked to be in her late teens. Over several dinners and long talks, we shared with each other stories and sorrows. I realized how difficult it must have been for a young woman to go through the centuries alone with no one to protect her. I was a man and a warrior but she was a small woman and although difficult to kill we still could feel pain and looking into her eyes, I could tell that she had felt many lifetimes worth of pain."

"What did she need your help for?"

Antonius slowly bowed his head, searching for the correct words and having found them, raised his head and looked directly into the eyes of the priest. "She wanted me to help her die."

"And did you?"

"Yes."

"How did it happen?"

He paused. "Since no one knows how she lived her life, I guess it is only fitting that the truth be told on how she ended her life."

The priest shifted position, and placed the Japanese sword on small table.

"Are you going to be using that today?"

"That is yet to be decided."

"Fair enough." He paused and then continued. "After about a week's sailing, we landed in Liverpool and spent the night in the finest hotel in the city. She ordered almost everything on the menu and savored each bite knowing that this would be one of her last meals. The next morning, we boarded a small schooner she had procured to take us to the city of Jaffa. After several days of sailing we landed in port and then took a short train ride to Jerusalem."

"Was this her first time back?"

"Yes. Too many memories, I guess." His gaze shifted as his mind replayed some distant recollection.

The priest tried to imagine what this man's life must have been like, all that he had seen, the history that he had lived. He was surprised to feel a wisp of envy float through his consciousness.

Antonius then continued. "We spent the next few days exploring Jerusalem but any resemblance to the city we once knew had long ago been destroyed. Hannah did find the parcel of land where her house had once stood. It had become a small apartment building and had a small garden that she had remembered playing in as a child. This was the first and only time that I ever saw her smile. As we stood there, she told me that this was where she wanted her ashes to be buried."

The Priest raised his eyebrows at hearing this. "Her ashes?"

"Yes, although the traditional Jewish custom is against the practice of cremation, Hannah no longer considered herself a traditional Jew. In fact, looking back at that time we spent together, I find it strange that we never once discussed religion." Antonius paused and then continued. "She had made arrangements to have complete and private access to a crematorium. On the last evening, we had what she called her 'last supper' in her hotel suite. The talk that night was surprisingly inconsequential and superficial. After dinner, we took two bottles of wine and walked to the crematorium. She had laced her bottle with heavy narcotics and sedatives, enough to kill a normal person. As we sat there in the parlor of the crematorium drinking, I was surprised that she asked me to hold her as she drifted off to sleep to face her final death. Maybe she saw me as her only connection to her past world, the present world, and possibly, the future world."

"She believed in heaven?" asked the priest.

"Maybe, I don't know. After she died and before she could regenerate, I placed her body into the fires of the crematorium and then stayed to collect the ashes when they had cooled. She had given me a small cedar box that she wanted her ashes to be placed in and then she had asked that the box to be buried in the garden. That was her last connection to the home she once knew. I did as she had asked, and after that, I became the last."

The priest said nothing for a long time as he absentmindedly traced the ornate carvings on the handle of the sword with his finger. After while he said, "That is some…story."

"So, isn't hard for a priest to murder someone?"

The question caught the priest off guard. "Murder?" he responded.

"Of course," Antonius responded. "Are you an officer of the court? Have I had a trial? A conviction? And what exactly am I being accused of?"

"Well…"

Antonius cut the priest off. "If you believe that your God is in control of everything, then I am just a helpless pawn playing my part on the cosmic chess board of life. If you believe in free will, then, again, I am innocent because my contamination was accidental and not of my own choosing. As I see it, you have but three choices."

The gaze of the priest now locked with that of Antonius.

Antonius continued. "One, you kill me and nothing happens and you discover that you have misinterpreted your Holy writings all these years. Two, you kill me and that ushers in the new Heaven and Earth. Three, you release me and allow me to slip back into the oblivion of the shadows."

The facial features of the priest became hard and focused. "You forgot the fourth option," the priest said coldly.

"The fourth option?" The priest thought he heard the slightest hint of fear in his captive's question.

The priest stood up and placed the Japanese sword on the table. He felt very old and very tired.

"Yes, the fourth option. I could just turn off the lights, and lock the door behind me."

Antonius exploded with rage and fear. "You fucking son of a bitch. I would rather die than be locked up in here. You are too gutless and don't have the balls to make a decision. Just kill me and see what happens."

The priest turned to face the door.

"Where is your faith, Priest?" Antonius spat out venomously. "Is this what your God wants or are you acting on your own fear?"

The priest slowly walked to the door.

Antonius shouted. "Revelations 3:16, 'So then, because you are luke-warm, and neither cold nor hot, I will spew you out of my mouth.' You are a fucking coward and a hypocrite." Antonius spat on the priest.

The hand of the priest hesitated on the door handle as he felt the warm spittle run down the back of his neck.

CONSTRUCTS

AS DARREN MCADAMS STOOD OUTSIDE OF THE RTR Construct building, he was experiencing a variety of emotions ranging from excitement to embarrassment, with a touch of shame. He patted his breast pocket feeling the gift card given to him by his friends on his 30th birthday party. Although, construct encounters were quite common and accepted in 2035, his conservative upbringing gave him lingering guilt.

The RTR Construct building was a very nondescript structure that could have easily passed for an insurance company. He took a deep breath and approached the door which opened automatically. The lobby was sparsely furnished with a few chairs and benches. Behind the reception desk sat an attractive young brunette. Dressed impeccably, as a top corporate lawyer would, with not a hair out of place, she was the visual definition of professionalism. At the sight of the young woman, Darren resisted the urge to turn around and leave. He hadn't expected this to be so awkward.

The young lady raised her eyes and looked at him. She smiled and said, "Welcome to RTR Constructs. I see by your actions that this is most likely your first time to participate in a construct experience."

Darren felt warmth rise through his neck as he felt a blush coming on.

"Uh, yes, it is."

"My name is Amy. I would like to assure you that we will do everything to make your experience as comfortable and satisfying as possible. All the information relating to your visit is strictly confidential. So how might I serve you today?"

Darren removed the gift card from his pocket and handed it to Amy.

"Oh, someone purchased you the premium package. They must think very highly of you." She smiled sweetly at him.

"It was a gift from my friends for my birthday."

"How delightful. Please take a seat and we will begin." At that, a padded seat arose from the floor and she motioned him to sit.

"Here at Realer Than Real Constructs, we endeavor to make your experience absolutely perfect and to do that we need to ask you some basic questions. Again, all your responses will be held in the strictest confidence. If you request, they can be destroyed after your experience. Most people keep them on file as it expedites the next visit, but that will be your decision. Let me bring up the configuration screen and we will begin."

Her melodic voice and continuous smile helped ease his nerves. His stomach still felt tied in knots and even though the ambient temperature was comfortable, he was aware of his body producing a significant amount of perspiration.

"All of our constructs are produced with the latest 3-D printer, using the finest medical grade silicones, for the most lifelike experience. Because of that, you have an infinite selection of constructs which you can design to meet your own wishes."

Darren furrowed his brow and slightly raise an eyebrow. "What do you mean, infinite selection?"

"Because of the on-site 3-D printer construction, you can have the gender of your choice as well as choosing race, height, body type, chest or breast size, as well as the general features such as hair and eye color. Since your friends purchased you the premium package, you also have the ability to have a construct printed for you that may reflect someone from the past."

"The past?" Darren queried.

"Yes, if you'd like a construct to look like a past movie star from the 1970s, such as Elizabeth Taylor or a supermodel from the 1990s, such as Heidi Klum, it can be provided. Or perhaps, you might desire to construct that looks like a teacher you might have had a crush on in the 10th grade. Due to the construct privacy laws, the only requirement is, if you desire a personalized construct, that the person must have been deceased for at least 10 years."

"Wow, this is much more complicated than I had expected."

"That is what makes RTR Constructs the premium construct experience. If this is too overwhelming for you, you can also start by looking at our most popular constructs."

"Yeah, let's start with that." Darren sighed with relief as a computer screen appeared from the reception desk. There were ten nude avatars of varying sizes and shapes. Darren eyes quickly settled on a petite female with short blond hair and piercing green eyes.

"I like number six," Darren said with some hesitancy and embarrassment.

"Excellent choice, sir. Now, would you like pubic hair or no pubic hair and if hair is desired, would you like natural, trimmed or styled," Amy asked with the smile that never faded.

"Styled?"

"Oh yes sir. You can choose from the Bermuda triangle, champagne glass, landing strip or postage stamp just to name a few. I can bring them up on the monitor if you'd like to see more options?"

"That's okay, trimmed will be fine" Darren mumbled nervously.

"Very good, sir." Without any hesitation, Amy continued. "Now for personality modifications. Using this slider bar on the computer screen, you can choose between personality number one who is demure and shy, to a number ten which is heavy into bondage and domination. I must inform you that any number above eight requires you to have a safe word which will be programmed into your personalized artificial intelligence program. Also, at that level, you will need to sign a waiver for health and safety reasons and to release RTR from any legal liabilities. If you choose constructs of one or two, your AI program will not have access to any of the more explicit or naughty language algorithms as they cause conflict with the underlying passive programming."

Darren looked at the slide bar and figured that a number five would be the place to start.

"A very wise choice, sir. A few more decisions and we will be ready to begin your construct build. Again, using the slide bar you can choose the level of sexual aggressiveness ranging from naïve and virginal, to aggressively oversexed."

Darren found that his embarrassment was quickly disappearing as it was remarkably easy to talk to Amy. "What is a five or six like?

"At this setting, the construct is very passionate, but she lets the man take the lead. She is very open about her own needs and will let the consumer know what experiences she desires if the consumer requests that information."

Darren slid the bar to six.

"Are we about done?"

"Yes, sir. I appreciate your patience; you have been such a pleasure to work with. Now, for the constructs voice, again you have almost unlimited choice of speech dialects and accents."

Darren was feeling more relaxed and at ease with the whole personal customization process. "How about a sexy French accent?"

"As you wish, sir. We are finished with the intake process. The printing of the construct will take approximately 20 minutes. You are welcome to have a seat in the lobby where refreshments will be provided as you desire."

"Thank you," Darren replied. "You have made this process a lot less awkward than I had imagined."

Amy looked at the desktop and then demurely raised her eyes to meet his gaze. Her head tilted slightly to one side. "Thank you, sir. Since you entered the lobby, I have been monitoring your respirations and heart rate as well as your stress pheromones. My responses and body language have all been programmed to reduce your own levels of stress. I am pleased that I have been successful."

"So, you're a…"

"Yes, sir. I am a construct. The fact you had to question this is a testament to the quality we strive to achieve here at RTR Constructs."

"Wow, okay. I'll just have a seat over here then. This is truly amazing. I think I'm going to have a great time."

"I'm sure you will, sir." Amy gave him a wink and a sly smile.

As Darren walked over to the couch, he began thinking of Ms. Kittredge, his 11th grade drama teacher who was his first big crush in life.

Maybe next time, he thought. Maybe next time.

COOKING TROLL

Dearest Hansel and Gretel,

Your uncle and I were so delighted to hear from you. We are so proud that you are doing well as you follow in the family business. The package that you sent arrived in good standing. I feel honored that you are asking for cooking advice from your old Aunt Nellie. The meats you sent presented quite an interesting quandary, but I feel I have devised some workable solutions.

When you first decided to start your own meat pie franchise using witches, I was at first skeptical the recipes I gave you would work with that type of meat. As you know, your Uncle Sweeney provides me with the finest gentleman of London who have been fatten on venison, bread pudding and rum. These make for succulent meat pies which have been my key to success. The fact that you two are running out of product is tribute to success of your enterprise and is very understandable as the number of witches is far less than the number of London gentleman.

So, let's get down to business. The packages of goblin and troll meats arrived packed on ice and in very good condition.

As you know, goblin meat is extremely stringy but surprisingly sweet. At first we tried using a new device called the Steam Digester which cooks with high pressure and steam. Unfortunately, these cooking devices have yet to be perfected and can sometimes explode, therefore your Uncle Sweeney forbade me from suggesting this to you as he would feel heartbroken if any harm befell you dear children. After much experimentation, I found that soaking goblin meat in a mixture of soured milk and sugar for 3-4 days softens the fibers and yields a delicious cut of meat. The meats should then be rinsed in sweet spring water before cooking into a pie. Goblin meat holds up well and therefore should only need a mild spice such as basil or rosemary.

Now to the troll meat. This was quite a challenge. When I opened the package, I thought the disgusting smell was a sign that the meat had become rancid, but I soon discovered this is the natural aroma of troll meat. The trouble with troll meat is, it is an extremely fatty meat. The key to working with this product is boiling, boiling and more boiling. Vinegar or wine, if available, is recommended. I suggest the process be performed in a shed away from the house as the odor can be overwhelming as discovered by the numerous complaints from Uncle Sweeney's paying barber customers.

After the boiling process is complete, the meat should be marinated in a mixture of fruit juices and wine. As fruit may be hard for you to obtain, tomato juice may be used as a substitute. This should occur in a cool dark place and the meat should be allowed to marinate for at least one week.

Although this is a time-consuming endeavor, the amount of meat you can obtain from one troll makes the process economical. Lastly, have Hansel take a meat mallet to the troll. This should provide the product with the gamey flavor, similar to wild duck, which should please your customers. Served with carrots, potatoes, and a sprig of sage make a surprisingly delightful treat.

As an interesting aside, we found that the tallow from the troll can be made into candles which, when lit in a cellar or barn, will drive out the rats. Uncle Sweeney found that when mixed with enough perfumes, the troll tallow makes a wonderful shaving soap which will soften the toughest of beards. We would be happy to purchase all of the excess troll tallow you might produce.

I hope these recipes will work for you.

It has been too long since we have seen our favorite niece and nephew. Hopefully, you can make it into the city for the holidays and we can swap more recipes. We love the both of you so very much.

Hugs,
Aunt Nellie Lovett
Uncle Sweeny Todd

EYE OF THE BEHOLDER

THE FIRST TRUE MEMORY THE BOY HAD WITH CLARITY AND conviction, that was factually sound, was of standing beside his mother's bed. She would arrange his clothes and smooth his hair and she would say,

"My perfect child, my perfect son, my perfect boy, my perfect one".

This was the morning ritual. His mother was not a strong woman, and therefore spent much of her time in her bedroom and a sitting room which were connected by two large oak doors with engravings the boy thought reminded him of Egyptian hieroglyphics.

After he made his morning appearance at his mother's bedside, he would then meet with various tutors in a small den lined with floor-to-ceiling bookcases, a fireplace and an oak table that could have comfortably sat four persons had there been a need. Light came from the curved windows at the top of the north and west walls, thus telling the boy that this was a corner room.

The boy enjoyed and endured a multitude of tutors in the subjects his father deemed the most important.

For the most part, the boy's studies followed the traditional path of reading, writing, mathematics, history and natural sciences. But then, every so often, and to what reason the boy could not understand, there could be short courses of study on seemingly unconnected topics such as herbal remedies, Native American weaving techniques, the history of glass blowing, and that of boxing or oriental forms of self-defense. He would take his courses in good stead, and sometimes he would try to predict which realm his next detour from traditional studies would take him. But, if there was a pattern behind his father's course selection, it was beyond his discernment.

All of his instructors commented on his remarkable hand writing, which was so precise it was sometimes confused with printed type. He enjoyed the structure of each letter, with each having its own exact configuration of lines, angles and curves.

His father was a moderately successful banker which fortuned them the luxury of living in a rambling Victorian home, a style popular in St. Louis at that time. With his father working long hours at the bank and his mother's seemingly endless states of fragile health, he spent most of his time in the care of nannies and various house servants.

It was in his tenth year when his mother's health took a deciding negative turn, bringing her near the edge of oblivion. But even then, he would start out every day at his mother's bedside to hear the words, sometimes in hardly more than a whisper,

"My perfect child, my perfect son, my perfect boy, my perfect one."

He was not acutely aware of when the idea first bubbled forth from somewhere deep in the childlike fantasy of his consciousness that there was a connection between his mother's health and his perfect control over his actions. It seemed logical to him that he could control the workings of the universe, or at least his mother's well-being, if he could be meticulously precise about certain mundane activities. It began with the tying of his shoelaces. He require that the length of the bow be the exact length of the loose tie. First, he re-laced each of his shoes so that each loose end was the exact length of the other. Each morning he would tie his shoes several times until the bow and the loose ends were identical in length.

Next, he began to walk down the exact center of the large oaken floored hallways which dominated his house. When some adult was met coming the other way, he would stop, staring at the harmony of his laces, until the adult would be forced to pass on the right or the left side of him. Often, while walking the exact center of the many corridors, he would overhear the servants making comments, "what a sad child," "what a pitiful boy."

Once he was confronted by two laborers who were in the process of bringing a new sofa to his mother's sitting room. As he saw the workers approach, he was aware of how out of order they seemed. One was a short, dark, stocky sort of a fellow with a large bushy mustache that was trimmed slightly shorter on the right side as compared to the left. His nails were chipped and broken, and there was dry, caked mud on his boots. Small pieces of dried mud flaked off as he walked, much like a pin oak tree shedding its mud brown colored leaves in winter.

The other man was taller, with a fair complexion and hue to his cheeks that reminded the boy of the color of peaches right before the time when they would reach their peak of sweetness. The boy quickly noted that the man's eyes seemed too closely spaced together in relation to the shape and conformity of his other features. Sad, he thought, to have to go through life with such an unbalanced face.

As the two workers and the small sofa approached, the boy stopped in the exact center of the hall and took his usual stance with his downward gaze. As the workers got closer, the taller fellow said in a joking sort of voice, "move to one side, young Master, befe you get squashed like a wee bug," in a thick brogue which betrayed an Irish heritage.

But the boy didn't move, despite the louder commands flying from the mouth of both workers. The two workers were forced to set the sofa on the wooden floor just inches away from the boy. "Are you deaf, Boy?" shouted the darker laborer with the unkempt nails. "Move to one side or the other." But the boy did not move.

The sound of the raised and heated voices brought the boy's nanny on to the scene, where, upon seeing the dilemma and knowing the boy, knew what her only recourse was. She placed her arms under the boy's arms and carefully lifted him to one side of the hallway where she gently placed him down and kept him there until the movers, mumbling in aggravation under their breath, and the sofa had safely passed. Then she lifted the boy and replaced him back in the center of the hallway. After making some small corrections to ensure he was centered, he continued on his journey.

The condition of his mother's health improved and at his heart's core, he was convinced that it was by his actions she had been restored and order brought back to his universe.

And then one day, a curious thing happened. He was looking through the *Sears and Roebuck* catalogue his father had received. His father used it on a regular basis so that he didn't have to perform the mandatory duties of purchasing household goods and personal items that his wife would have performed had she been in better health. The boy would place the book on the center of the table in the room where his lessons took place, precisely halfway between each of the table's corners. Then slowly, and with great deliberation, he would reach his left hand over to grasp the upper right corner of the page as he would turn pages with the reverence of dealing with the Holy Book or the unrolling of the Torah.

It was during one of these catalog explorations that his eye happened to wander to a line drawing of a petite young woman combing her hair while looking at her reflection in a mirror. She had long curls and was dressed in a manner to suggest she was getting ready to retire or had just awoken from a night of blissful sleep. A question formed in his mind, as if that last dot of a connect-the-dots puzzle had been completed. As best he could recall, he had never seen a mirror in his home, yet from the magazine he was able to deduce that it was somewhat common to have mirrors in private dressing rooms and bathing areas as well as in entry ways and hallways. Still he had never seen a mirror in his house and as he pondered further, he began to realize that he had never seen a clear reflection as to the true nature of his own features. He had seen distorted images in silver trays or a highly polished flat knife, but he had never seen his own reflection in the clarity of a mirror.

He recalled seeing the female house staff draw forth small compacts of bronze or tortoise shell from their dress pockets or purses. They would examine their face and apply powder or blush, as the occasion required, before leaving the house for the periodic trip to the market or to perform some other household errand. He began to dwell in curiosity on the absence of mirrors in his home. His mother had beautiful, yet frail features that reminded him of the porcelain ballerinas decorating several small tables in the house. He had once remarked to her how she looked as beautiful as the tiny figurines and was rewarded with a warm and bountiful smile and embrace.

She had whispered in his ear,

"My perfect child, my perfect son, my perfect boy, my perfect one."

She had kissed him on the cheek and he still recalled the tingling sensation he'd felt as her warm, sweet breath floated over and into his ear like molasses. Whenever he recalled the event, he was aware of having a sensation which he could neither identify nor explain. Curious, he thought.

His father's features included a precisely trimmed mustache and eyebrows, since he would not permit a bushy face. His piercing eyes reminded the boy of the elegant gentlemen he had seen on the tins of tobacco advertised in his beloved *Sears and Roebuck* catalogue.

His mother was angelically beautiful and his father had strong and fine features, so what, he wondered, was the need to keep mirrors out of the house? And then it struck him, the hairs on the back of his neck tingled as they did when one of his teachers was demonstrating the principle of static electricity. It must be *him*. There must be something so hideously wrong with this face that his beloved parents had gone to such extreme measures to protect him from seeing himself.

So, he began the quest to find a mirror. At first, he thought that he would try to sneak one from a female house servant, but they always locked their bags in small wooden cabinets in the pantry. He reasoned his father must have one since he would need it to keep his mustache so neatly trimmed. But his father's bedroom and bath also included a study where he kept many important work-related papers, so he would always lock his door whenever he would leave to begin his duties at the bank. From what the boy could gather from his trusted *Sears and Roebuck* catalogue and his own observations, women used mirrors frequently and they were likely to be found in the bath or dressing area.

His first inclination was that he would just ask his mother to look at a mirror, but then he reasoned, if they were purposefully denying his access to mirrors, that she would obviously deny his request. And now, thus alerted, would make extra efforts to deny him his prize. No, he thought, this quest must occur with such great stealth as to not alert his parents to its existence or conclusion.

His mother often kept her door slightly ajar since she felt her room was too stuffy without a crosscurrent of air. Her habit, as it were, was to take an afternoon nap on a frequent, if not daily basis. This, he reasoned, would be the time to achieve his goal. He waited until Sunday when most of the house staff were off to be with their own families. Also, the midday meal was usually grander than the weekdays and more likely to ensure that his mother would soon be napping.

About three quarters of an hour after he saw the servants remove his mother's serving tray, he began his purposeful march down the center of the hallway to his mother's room. As he reached the door, he unlaced his meticulously tied shoes and placed them behind on a low table just outside his mother's room as to obscure them from the observation of a casual passerby. He then opened her door with care and listened to her breathing, which he found to be reassuringly slow and regular. He stepped in on socked feet to see her lying quietly on her right side facing away from the door. He stood a moment without moving and scanned the room to convince himself he was truly alone. After a few moments, he felt assured his mother was sleeping and also that he heard no sounds of servants' shoes in the hallway.

There was a small door off of the sitting room he assumed must be the entryway to his mother's private bathing area, and if he were to find a mirror, this is where it would be. Slowly and with great deliberateness, he walked to the door using the small gliding steps he had learned during his oriental defense studies. An instructor had told him that these were the movements needed if one wanted to move quietly like a cat walking on silk.

As he reached the door, he noticed his heart was pounding and moisture dominated his palms. Did he really want to see what so much effort had been put forth to keep from him? Could he handle the sight of his deformity which he imagined must dominate his facial features? With these thoughts rushing through his brain, he slowly turned the handle of the door that would forever change his life.

GIGGLY GOOD

AS THE PROTEOLYTIC ENZYMES BEGAN THE PROCESS OF digesting her body, Kat thought back to a winter vacation she'd spent with her Uncle Joe in Grand Forks, North Dakota. He'd once used the term 'giggly good' which she was unfamiliar with, and he explained this was a sensation so utterly delightful; it made a person giggle uncontrollably. To demonstrate this, he had her turn the electric blanket on her bed to the highest setting for several minutes. He then had her change into her pajamas and invited her stand outside in the snow until she was so cold that she was shaking. Then she ran back to her bed and dove into the warm cocoon comfort of her bed. She smiled and giggled uncontrollably. She now understood. Giggly good.

It was a stupid rookie mistake. Kat, only her Uncle called her Kathryn, had come from a long lineage of Bioprospectors. She remembered stories about her grandmother going into the Amazon rain forest in search of plants that could be used in foods, cosmetics, and medicines. It had become big business until the end of the 21st century. Approximately seventy-eight percent of all new medications are based on plant, fungi, animal or bacterial sources. Her grandmother, and later her father, had been a part of the plant biology gold rush which attempted to identify and save as many medicinal plants as possible before the destruction of all natural rain forests on Earth.

So it was only natural Kat had been harvesting mucous off of the surface of a large gelatinous life form the locals called a *slug bug* when the accident occurred.

She'd started out early in the morning to harvest as the planet, Epsilon 5, had a binary sun which kept the humidity Amazon thick and heavy. Dressed in a light khaki shirt and shorts, which was already matted to her body, sweat rolled off all exposed skin.

Not keeping her eye on the terrain, she'd carelessly tripped over a rock and fell into the jelly like slug bug. The name 'slug bug' came from an old earth reference to the Volkswagen Beetle, circa 1960, which was similar in shape and size to this alien species. It was a simple creature, part animal, part plant, and it survived by attracting its prey with seductive scents. Once the prey came into contact with the slug bug, neurotransmitters were secreted that placed the captive into a state of instant euphoria so it wouldn't struggle as the slug bug engulfed it and began the process of digestion.

Collecting the mucous coating of the slug bug was very profitable since it could be processed into several psychoactive medicinal compounds which were useful for treating depression, space psychosis, as well as several other psychological ailments. There were also black market uses for the slug bug's slime based on its innate ability to induce a state of ecstasy.

As she closed her eyes, she was unaware of her skin being eaten away, exposing muscle, tendon, and bone. She was unaware of the feeling of suffocation as the mucous covered her face. She was only vaguely aware of her impending death. The feeling of total bliss and euphoria filled her entire consciousness. She had one last thought as she drifted into unconsciousness.

"Giggly good," Kat thought. "Yes, giggly good."

GROUPON 2050

SIX Hand Robotic Massage

Call now to schedule your SIX hands Robotic Massage™. We have the latest in Humaform robotics to ensure your robotic massage is indistinguishable from human hands.

Choose from over **TWENTY** different massage styles including Swedish Massage Therapy, Deep Tissue Massage, Shiatsu Massage, Thai Massage, Pregnancy Massage or Reflexology, just to name a few. Happy Ending Massage (legal in all 50 states except Utah). Select hand temperature as well as pressure sensation desired.

** This week only, all packages are ½ price

** 60-Minute Swedish Massage- only .05 Bitcoin

** 60-Minute Couple's Swedish Massage- only .80 Bitcoin

Two Week Moon Vacation!

Travel and Lodging Included

Enjoy a three-day flight on board the Grand Voyager or the Grand Celestial space liner! You will be amazed at the number of activities you can pack into your 3-night stay aboard one of the finest space liners, as ranked by Travel Magazine! Enjoy multiple on-board restaurants with a view of the Cosmos or private meals in your luxurious cabin. Spend your days relaxing in our finest automated spa as you are attended by state of the art AI service bots (pleasure bots not included). In the evening, you'll have your choice from an exciting mix of casinos, or take in talented performers as they amaze you with their low gravity acrobatics!

Once on the moon, you'll have 7 days at the newly opened Lunar Hyatt. The newest of the Hyatt jewels, this resort hotel goes above and beyond with detail-oriented personal service. Spend your days exploring the Eagle Lunar Museum and schedule a trip to the original landing site. Or, rent a moon buggy and enjoy exploring the local moonscape on your own. Guided tours are also available. You may also decide to take advantage the moons 1/6 gravity as you take suited walks outside.

Options include -

- 14 day round trip transportation aboard the Grand Voyager or the Grand Celestial space liner in an interior or space-view cabin with all meals (excluding specialty dining options), on board live entertainment and kids programs supervised by the latest NannySafe ® AI bots - "Safer than leaving your children with their Grandmother."

- Discounted fees vary due to solar flares, space debris cycles and fluctuations in fuel costs. Please call for the latest updates.

We accept all cyber currency as well as gold bullion and of course.... PayPal.©

Weight Watcher's Virtual Chef ™

Weight loss has never been easier!

With Weight Watchers™ new premium home edition of its breakthrough patented All Senses Virtual Chef, you can lose weight without exercise, chemical liposuction, or gastric contents exchange. With the invention of the Micro Array Sensory Input ™, you can now have all the sensations of sight, smell, sound and of course….. TASTE!

The Virtual Chef is programmed with over **10,000** foods from every culture and cuisine on Earth, as well as the outer planets. Imagine having all of the culinary sensations ranging from your favorite hamburger and mushroom pizza to a succulent Fourchu lobster drenched in drawn honey butter with a side order of Almas caviar all while eating less than 100 calories of Weight Watcher's vitamin enriched soy faux food!

The results will amaze you as you can eat an unlimited number of calories in virtual food while taking in **only 500 calories** of faux food. You'll finally have the body you always dreamed of having!

After you have imprinted your neural scan onto the Virtual Chef, you will be ready to indulge yourself in guiltless culinary delights. The process is easy! Simply place the Virtual Chef on your head, set the dial for any of the 10,000 foods, then pick the appropriate faux meals. Then enjoy! You can also program your own variations allowing you to relive and enjoy your Grandmother's banana cream pie or your Mother's famous fried chicken!

The Virtual Chef has a built-in safety feature warning you if your weight loss drops below a BMI of 19 and the machine will automatically cease to function if your BMI drops below 17.5. Weight Watchers is not responsible for the cost of acquiring a new wardrobe due to weight loss.

Losing weight has never been this easy.

Call for our special couples pricing.

GYNO TO THE STARS

"PLEASE HARNESS YOURSELF IN AS WE MAKE PREPARATION for docking at the United Nations Space Station," the doctor heard over the scratchy intercom.

Space travel was not as glamorous as he had imagined. As he sat listening to the unfamiliar and not so reassuring groans and creaks of the military transport craft, he thought about the series of decisions he'd made resulting in him speeding 74,600,000 miles from Earth.

The first decision was to apply to medical school. After acceptance, he was tasked with finding a way to pay for medical school. When the Navy recruiter offered him the finances to cover six years of books, tuition, and living expenses, he jumped at the opportunity. In return, he promised to repay the Navy by serving as a physician. At the end of the deployment, he would be debt free. His plan was to return to his home town of Los Angeles where he hoped to have a practice dealing with the rich and famous as an obstetrician/gynecologist. He would joke with his friends that he wanted to be the 'Gyno to the Stars". This was the second critical decision.

The third critical decision was taking the elective course in xenobiology, or as the students called it, Aliens 101, which was a cursory discussion of alien pathophysiology of the numerous species humans had encountered while exploring the galaxy. Since there was very little known about alien pathophysiology, the class had the reputation as being an easy A.

After completing his residency, he shined his brand-new Lieutenant bars and excitedly joined the staff of the naval hospital in San Diego, one of the most coveted deployments available. Life was good.

The last and most disastrous decision he made was when, while playing golf, he got a call that a Captain's wife was in the ER with the complaints of vaginal itching. In his youthful arrogance, he decided that vaginal itching was not an emergency and waited to finish his round of golf before heading to the hospital. He reasoned that no one ever died from a yeast infection.

As a result of that decision, he now found himself breathing in the stale air of a military transport somewhere out by Saturn's moon, Titan. He had learned a valuable lesson about power and authority. His two Lieutenant bars were no match for the wings of the Captain.

The UNSS had the distinction of having the only tertiary medical center in the outer planets and hosted a human population of about 3,000 and a nonhuman operation of about half that.

Many of the alien cultures had their own medical personnel on the station, since numerous habitats had to be simulated to accommodate special needs. Some clinics catered to aquatic life forms while others were self-contained gaseous atmospheres. Before the invention of the universal translator, there had been near disastrous encounters due breakdowns in communication.

His briefing packet had described the station as having a central core which housed propulsion, administration and maintenance. Surrounding the core were many circular rings which were home to the majority of the human and non-human population. It was a monstrous structure measuring over two miles in length.

The crackle of the intercom announced they'd docked and he was free to leave the craft. He grabbed his pack that had been tethered to the bulkhead and walked to the airlock along with all of the other arriving passengers. Most were human but he recognized an avian being from Regis 5 with its bright red head plume and a short, stocky creature resembling a large hedgehog from the outer quadrant. Everything was unfamiliar. The mixed odors, the artificial gravity, the fruit salad of alien life; he felt overwhelmed.

Once outside the airlock, he was met by an older woman with dark brown hair. Short and tight as was naval regulations. She had striking features, piercing green eyes and identified herself as Major Barbara Penland, his head nurse and manager of the OB/GYN department.

"Sorry to break you in like this Doc, but we have a Borlac in active labor. No time for a tour. We have to hurry," she said as she led him away from the other passengers.

"A Borlac?" he asked over his shoulder, as Major Penland pushed their way through the crowded corridor. He was experiencing sensory overload and was feeling a little light headed. Things were happening too fast.

"Yes, a Borlac. They said you were trained in xenobiology."

"I only had one introductory course as a medical student."

The Major looked obviously exasperated with a deep furrowed brow and made no effort to hide her feelings. "Well crap. Isn't that just like the military to screw things up. Too late for that now. Do you remember anything about Borlac physiology of labor?"

"No, not really."

"Double crap. The Borlacs look like something between a giant lizard and a rhinoceros. Gentle beings except when they're in active labor. Then they revert back to a more primitive behavior pattern, much like an unmedicated human labor."

He didn't know if she was trying to make a joke.

"For this delivery you will go enter in a padded gown and wearing a hazmat suit because of the stench."

"Whoa, time out. Padded gown? Hazmat suit?"

"Damn it, Doc. You really don't know shit, do you? The Borlac have a tendency to kick when they hit active labor, so you'll be dressed in a special padded gown. They can kick like a mule"

He was almost afraid to ask about the hazmat suit.

"The Borlac have developed an evolutionary defense mechanism to protect the mother and her infant from predators. When she gets close to delivery, she will expel the most foul smelling slime from glands near her birth canal. Think of the most disgusting, gut retching smell you can imagine. Multiply it by a thousand and you will only get close to what the odor is really like. We have to deliver Borlacs in the decontamination unit because it has a closed air circulation unit."

Every cell in his body sounded a warning as he suddenly had the urge to turn and run screaming back to the docking craft.

Major Penland walked him to the physician's dressing room where he put down his pack as she showed him how to assemble the padded surgical gown. It looked like a combination between the protective gear of Earth football and a bomb disposal suit.

"Next you put on the hazmat suit. It's too early to put on the headgear yet."

His mind was spinning. It was like being on an out-of-control roller coaster. Things were moving too fast. Lumbering towards labor and delivery, he felt like a large snowman and wondered how he was ever going to be able to perform a delivery dressed as he was.

At that moment he heard a large rumbling roar and was overwhelmed by a smell that required all of his willpower not to expel his stomach contents.

Major Pendland snapped her own headgear into place. "She sounds like she is getting close, Doc. Time to suit up."

* * * * * *

Later, as he was dictating a delivery note, the major offered him a cup of coffee.

"You did good, Doc. How do you feel?"

"Well, I have a bruised shoulder and possibly a cracked rib," he said, trying to look stoic. "I've never delivered a 30 pound infant before and you could have warned me about the Borlac birthing plan. I was kinda caught off guard when the patient wanted to chew through her umbilical cord and eat her placenta immediately after delivery."

"Oh, yeah. Sorry. I guess I forgot to mention that," replied the major with a sly smile on her face. "When you finish with your dictation, I'll show you to your quarters. We have a long day of clinic and orientation tomorrow."

As he sat there alone watching the steam from his coffee making unusual patterns due to the artificial gravity, he thought to himself, "Gyno to the Stars. Yep, that's me. Gyno to the stars.

HOW SMALL

(Written at age 13)

A SMALL BUNDLED FIGURE STOOD, LOOKING ACROSS THE cold desolate land. It had been a frozen land ever since he could remember, but of course Myton was only six. He looked at the one huge structure that the entire Creatan civilization lived in. Its large triangular walls glowed with the heat that kept his people alive. He wondered if he would live to see any change, for any temperature would be better than this.

* * *

YEARS LATER, HE LOOKED AROUND AT THE HUNDREDS OF buildings connected by many thin and fragile looking roads that seemed to float in midair. Myton remembered the day the temperature started to rise. He was glad he had lived through the Great Freeze; many of his people had not survived. He was twenty-two now and he had lived to see his race make great progress.

HE LOOKED UP AT THE CEILING OF THE MEDICAL STATION; IT was the only building left standing when the heat came. He knew that the mighty Creatan civilization was coming to an end. Myton and the last members of his race were lying on the floor dying. At age fifty-three, he had lived through the Great Freeze and the Time of Peace, but they could not stand up against the blistering heat which had brought destruction to his world.

FOUR MEN IN WHITE COATS STOOD AROUND A PRONE FIGURE lying on the table. Dr. Harris looked at Dr. Forester. "What happened?" he asked. "I thought he was going to recover."

Their patient was Major William B. Matter, one of the first men to go to Mars. Dr. Forester didn't know why the astronaut had died. From the reports he'd read, the Mars Landing Party had been going well when they'd radioed to Earth that they had discovered small life on Mars and were returning home immediately. Soon after liftoff, a rogue meteor had torn through the hull, fatally injuring the biochemist as well the rest of the crew.

The Major, realizing the seriousness of his injuries, had punctured the leg of his auto-repairing space suit. The self-sealing seams had isolated his leg from the rest of his body, but his leg was frozen stiff in the vacuum. He'd been rushed to the hospital as soon as the craft had landed. On the way he kept mumbling incoherently that he'd brought the Martian life back with him, but had fallen unconscious before he could say anymore. The military and scientists had searched everywhere but hadn't found the life-form he'd mentioned. They assumed it was the ranting of a fevered brain.

The doctors had then bathed the leg in warm water to slowly thaw it out. The cells had responded and they thought he was going to live. All of a sudden, he had developed a high fever and died within a couple of hours.

Dr. Forester wondered if there was small life on Mars, but he never realized how small life could be, for, deep inside the cells of the astronaut's leg the last of the Creatan civilization, was dying.

HOWLING AT THE MOON

THEY WERE THROWN TOGETHER LIKE TWO UNWITTING PAS-
sengers now huddled together for comfort and support on a lifeboat,
watching as the Titanic sank. In this case, the Titanic was named Mike,
and in one tragically painful moment, the girl of ten lost her father and the
man lost his best friend, his brother, the keeper of his dreams and inner
demons. The girl and the man had been aware of each other as Venus is
aware of Mars and, as such, traveled separate orbits around a central Sun.
Their interactions had been transient and shallow in nature. They knew of
each other but did not know each other.

She was an ethereal creature, mysterious and driven by forces beyond
his experience as he had been the father of two sons.

Time moved on, but normal was never normal again. She withdrew
from the onslaught of well-intended but prying questions.

How are you feeling?

Are you all right?

Do you want to talk about it?

With each question she pulled further into her shell and found solace in the only escape which asked nothing of her...books. She found when she had a book open or its electronic counterpart on her lap, people tended to stay away. Books became her "Do Not Disturb" sign.

After the death of Mike, the man had cut back on his hours of work as to be more available to his friends' family.

One of the first traditions to start had been picking the girl up from school for Wednesday night church services.

In the beginning, she'd wanted to sit in the back seat as it made her feel safe and reminded her of how life used to be. The man didn't like this. It made him feel they were acting out a scene from *Driving Miss Daisy*. But she was stubborn, and that was where she would stay. In the beginning they had nothing in common other than their love of Mike. He made tentative probes into the defenses of her heart's fortress trying to find a point of entry into her life. They found their commonality was a love of science fiction and rock music of the 70's, interests Mike had instilled into his daughter at an early age.

One day, early in their developing relationship, she asked him how she could be sure it was, in fact, him picking her up from school. She wove very clever scenarios from alien shape shifters to kidnappers wearing rubber facemasks to look like him. At first, he thought she was just being a playful, goofy 10-year-old. But, as he thought about the question in more depth, he understood she was asking him a deeper one.

Can I trust you?

So, they developed a secret sign, a salute, identifying one to the other. Soon after that, she moved to the front seat of the Lexus, which soon became the place where secrets would be shared, school dramas played out, and she would grow into a teenager.

This is how their relationship began, tentative at first like a toddler walking on new legs.

This was the beginning of their new reality.

In the beginning, she reminded him of a turtle who'd spent much of her time within her shell and only on rare occasions did she venture forth. She didn't like to take chances, because chances meant change. With the death of her father, and her mother withdrawing into the shadows of grief, she felt as if she'd had enough change to last a lifetime.

Since she had no control over the large aspects of her life, she sought to exert her own control over smaller issues. She found security and comfort within the walls of routine. For months, after school meals were either Arby's or Taco Bueno, no exceptions, no deviations.

And then one day, he suggested an experiment, and at the mention of the word "experiment," the turtle peeked her head out just a little. Luckily, she was more curious than cautious. He explained every week they would eat at different food establishments between her school and the church he took her to on Wednesday evenings. No matter how fancy or plain, if they passed it, they would stop and try the food. This was the first crack the turtle allowed in her shell.

For the first two years after her father's death and her mother's isolation, she was filled with anger. She and the man had many long talks about the concept of anger being a secondary emotion. He told her a person always feels a primary emotion before they feel the anger, and understanding comes from identifying that primary emotion. But for most people, even children, feeling anger was safer – it was a wall of protection.

She was filled with many primary emotions, as numerous as the number of colors in a box of crayons. Sadness at the loss of her daddy. Loneliness at the understandable, but nevertheless, emotional abandonment of her mother. Fear at the loss of the stabilizing gyroscope which kept her family in harmony. Self-imposed guilt brought on by imaginary sins she'd never committed. And, as if this wasn't enough, Mother Nature threw in the normal angst coming with the change of mind, body, and emotions as one transitions from a youthful child to a budding adolescent.

As he watched her, he often felt as if he were an anthropologist secretly observing the culture and habits of an unknown tribe or a recently discovered lifeform. He was amazed how everyday brought subtle changes that would go unnoticed to the casual observer.

They then discovered they both had a love of music. The man played the guitar, and she was learning to play the piano. She loved to sing, although only to herself. Some of her favorites were her dad's favorite songs such as, "House of the Rising Sun" and "Werewolves of London." Often, when they were driving, she would ask to connect his phone to the car's audio system so she could listen to the "Classics."

He tried often to get her to sing along with him but, at most, a soft whisper would escape her lips.

It was a warm summer's evening, two years later, when things changed. As they were driving back home late at night, the moon was full, and the sweet smell of summer was in the air. He opened the moon roof and the heat of the Oklahoma summer flowed over them like warm molasses.

> *I saw a werewolf with a Chinese menu in his hand,*
> *Walking through the streets of Soho in the rain.*
> *He was looking for the place called Lee Ho Fook's,*
> *Going to get a big dish of beef chow mein.*
> *Ahhwooooo... Werewolves of London, Ahwooooo!*
> *Ahhwooooo... Werewolves of London, Ahwooooo!*

When the chorus came around he said, "Give me a loud 'Ahwooooo!'"

She looked at him and said nothing.

"Come on. It's a beautiful night with a full moon and if we don't howl, the werewolves will get us."

As the next chorus came around, she let out a squeak of an *Ahwooooo!*

"No," he insisted. "Dig deep. Take a deep breath and let out a loud Ahwooooo!" He lifted his head and demonstrated by howling at the moon.

This time, the *Ahwooooo!* was better, but not even close to the howl he wanted.

"That's better, but I want the moon to hear you. Howl like you mean it!"

She stared at the iPhone she was holding in her lap and gave him a sideways glance. He knew she was pondering the action.

And then, someplace deep inside her, the dam of insecurity and self-consciousness broke loose. Like a pearl diver straining to reach the surface before the breath of life ran out, all the while holding on to her precious cargo, an *'Ahwooooo'* was bubbling up from the depths. She lifted her head and howled at the moon and at that moment, he knew she would be okay. The worst had passed, and just as a hopeful, healing spring always follows the depressive cold of winter, he knew she was ready to begin the process of letting go and moving on.

Months later, beaming a smile capable of melting a Frost Giant's heart, she coyly confessed she had been practicing her howl, just in case the need arose.

What started as an obligation, turned into much more. She became the daughter he never had and, through loving her, he continued to honor and love his best friend. She, in turn, had a person serving as a connection to the stories and passions of her father's life. The stories and embellishments helped keep her father's memory alive. Together they helped each other to heal, to grow, and have the strength to go on.

And now, whenever they see a full moon, it reminds them there are times in life when howling at the moon is sometimes the only thing you can do.

NEVER TRUST A TROLL

THEDUR SAT HUDDLED WITH A BURLAP SACK OVER HIS HEAD trying to shield himself from the near deafening buzzing. He should have known better as he remembered words his grandmother used to say to him:

"Never trust a troll."

The county his family lived in unfortunately had a large troll population. They lived in brier patches, under bridges, in caves, and they would call out to unwary travelers in the hopes of engaging them in conversation. Conventional wisdom was to ignore them as a troll was sly in its ability to manipulate even the brightest person. Thedur had been diligent in avoiding trolls until one warm summer's morning when he was crossing the old stone bridge traversing a dry stream bed on his way into town.

He hurried over the bridge, as bridges made him nervous, when he heard someone call out for help from underneath. Fearing some other traveler had fallen from the bridge which was old and in disrepair with many loose stones, he hurried down the bank to provide assistance.

What he found, much to his surprise, was a troll whose leg was trapped under a stone. He had seen trolls before from a distance but never up close. They were much uglier than he'd imagined, with beady little eyes and hair growing out of parts of the body where it never was intended to be. The troll had cartoonishly large ears and a nose that seemed to provide an endless cascade of green thick mucus.

"Help me," pleaded the troll. "Help me and you will be rewarded."

The troll was in obvious pain, but his grandmother's warning flashed in his brain. *Never trust a troll.*

"Please," the troll whined as he wiped a hairy arm across his dripping nose, an arm that was already crusted over with a thick layer of old dried snot.

"Okay, I'll remove the stone, but after that I'm out of here," Thedur replied, his voice shaking.

"Thank you, you are so kind." With that, the troll began to sob in a way that reminded Thedur of a small child.

Thedur looked around; half-expecting some type of trap, but it was just him and the pitiful troll. He then, with significant effort, lifted the large stone holding the troll captive. As he lifted, the troll quickly pulled his leg free, rolled away, and started rubbing his bruised appendage.

"Thank you, oh, *thank you.*" gushed the troll. "I was afraid I would die beneath this bridge".

"Well, I'm glad you're okay," said Thedur, as he began to climb up the bank and continue his journey into town.

"Wait," implored the troll. "I haven't given you your reward."

"I didn't do this for the reward. I'm sorry but I have got to go." His grandmother's warning of *never trust a troll* kept rolling around his brain, and he was anxious to get away.

"But don't you even want to hear what the reward is?"

Thedur knew he shouldn't, but he did. He paused and turned back to the troll.

It wouldn't hurt just to listen, he thought.

The troll's eyes seem to twinkle mischievously as he dug into an old bag he had slung around his shoulder. He pulled out a small vial of brownish liquid that he placed on a rock in front of Thedur.

"Here it is," said the troll as he looked at Thedur expectantly. "Oh, I see you do not trust me. We trolls have never understood how we got the reputation for being untrustworthy."

Thedur just looked at the vial sitting on the rock in front of him, half expecting it to explode or summon forth some type of monster. He hesitated before asking, "What does it do?"

"What does it do? What does it *do*? Let me tell you what it does," the troll said, as he clapped his hands excitedly. "Do you have a piece of silver or gold on you?"

Without thinking, Thedur reached into his pocket to feel two small silver coins he had there. He nodded to the troll.

"Good, it is very simple. First, you place the coins on the flat rock in front of you. Then you rub the liquid from the vial onto your hands being very careful not to touch anything until you are ready. This is very important."

"Why?" asked Thedur.

"Because, the first thing you touch, you will receive an amount of that item every morning. The amount will be equal to your own weight." The troll looked Thedur up and down and said, "You weigh about ten stones?"

"I guess," mumbled Thedur.

"So, every morning when you wake up, you would have a pile of silver equal to ten stones which you can use for the rest of the day. When you sleep, the silver would disappear but return every morning for as long as you live."

Thedur could sense this was a trap and knew he should leave, but he didn't think it would hurt to ask a few questions.

"If I buy something with the silver, will that stay with me?"

"Yes," replied to troll.

"If I pay for services from a merchant or a workman with the silver, will it remain in their pocket when I sleep?"

"Most certainly," replied the troll.

"What if I want to buy gold with my silver? Will the gold still be there in the morning?"

"No," replied the troll who was beginning to sound somewhat annoyed. "Magic knows when you are not being true to the spell."

"But, if I buy a large house and land, those will be with me when I wake up in the morning. Right?"

"Yes, yes, yes," answered a perturbed troll.

Thedur thought about his next move very carefully. He removed the two silver coins from his pocket and placed them carefully on the flat stone. There was nothing between the silver coins and himself. Slowly, and with great caution, he picked up the vial and removed the cork sealing its contents. The voice of his grandmother was silenced by expectation and greed. When he was confident that nothing would interfere with his touching the silver coins, he poured the liquid over his hands.

At that exact moment, a fly tried to land on his nose and without thinking, he swatted the fly which went spinning away dizzily.

Immediately, he was surrounded by millions of flies, the weight of ten stones. He had never seen so many flies and the buzzing sound they made was deafening. He quickly pulled out a burlap sack which he had brought to carry home his purchases from the town store and placed it over his head. He could feel flies swarming around him, he could feel them crawling up his pant legs and getting inside his shirt.

"You tricked me!" he screamed at the troll.

"I did not. Everything happened exactly like I said it would. You are the one that who swatted a fly instead of touching the silver," answered the troll as he started to leave and head back into the darkness of the underbrush.

"Take the spell off of me," cried Thedur in anguish.

"What is done, cannot be undone," quipped the troll.

"What am I supposed to do?" pleaded Thedur.

As the troll slipped into the shadows of the thicket, he shouted over his shoulder to Thedur. "Do? *Do*? That I cannot say, but maybe next time you should listen to your grandmother."

NINE SILLY ELECTRONS

(Written at age 14)

THINGS AT THE PALOMAR OBSERVATORY WERE NOT QUIET. Deep within the great walls of the building that housed the huge telescope, Dr. John Werter was hastily re-checking his calculations. Utter horror and disbelief played on his face, because he had just discovered that, not only the world but the entire universe was coming to an end.

It had started six days ago when he'd noticed the deep darkness of space he'd become accustomed to viewing, seemed to be getting lighter. At first he'd thought it was his imagination, but when he checked his light meter that measured brightness or lumens, he found the darkness of space was definitely getting lighter, as if some gigantic light were moving toward the world. Within a matter of hours, he'd conferred with other astronomers around the world and found they too had noticed the lighter sky. That had been the first day.

The second day came. The sky was still getting lighter, and no explanation appeared. He had received a phone call from Washington requesting his participation in a high-level government meeting on the phenomenal brightening of the sky. Reluctantly, he'd agreed to attend, for you could not turn down the president. Dr. Werter could tell them nothing, for he knew nothing as to the cause of the brightening of the sky except it was definitely getting lighter. He would have rather stayed at the observatory where he might have done some good.

He arrived at the capital on the third day where he was met by a government official. Once at the hotel, the official handed Dr. Werter a keycard to his assigned room and informed him to stay in his room until it was time to report to the conference later in the day.

When he opened the door to the meeting room, he saw some of the most brilliant minds of his time. There was astrophysicist Dr. Phom of Thailand and Dr. Asderski of Moscow, the leader in theoretical physics, among the many other men and women from all areas of science. Seated with the group was what appeared, to Dr. Werter, to be a strong military presence. The meeting went on late into the night, with very little being accomplished, for everyone knew the sky was getting brighter but no one knew how or why or what consequences it might have on the world. Speculations ran rampant.

By the end of the fourth day, when it was decided there was nothing they could do at this point, the meetings concluded. They all needed more data and returned to their respective institutions to continue the research. Dr. Werter took the first available transportation back to the observatory. Even without the telescope, he could tell the sky was now even brighter. Though it was the middle of the night, the sky looked like early dawn.

The sounds of shouting and horns blaring woke him the next morning. Looking out his window, he saw a small army of news vans and reporters being held up at the observatory's gate. He turned on the cable news and saw the reason why. The news tag read: IS THE WORLD COMING

TO AN END? SCIENTISTS STUMPED. Panic was spreading through the world like wildfire. Scenes from around the world showed everything from rioting to enormous religious gatherings. He opened up his email inbox to find it full of requests for information and confirmation.

The one from the White House read:

Scientists from Eastern Europe report the universe is coming to an end. Please respond at the soonest possible moment.

He sent one of his assistants to tell the reporters that he had no comment to make.

He went to the telescope, but in daylight all he could see was a brilliant white light. He would have to wait until midnight so he could make a reading when the Earth was turned away from the oncoming light.

He tried to get some sleep to prepare for the night, but only succeeded in dozing in and out of consciousness. When Dr. Werter awoke it was a little past midnight. It was very hard to believe all of this had started just six days ago. He didn't have time to think on that now, so he went to the telescope to begin taking readings. Where he had expected to see the comforting twinkle of stars, he saw only light. He checked again for he had to be sure.

The stars were gone. Millions of stars with planets circling around them were no longer in existence; gone, as if they had never existed. In a stunned daze he walked to the computer and sent an email confirming the universe, without any known reason, was coming to an end. It was as if the white light had started at the far end of the universe and was now cutting through it from one end to the other. On the seventh day, his own solar system would be blotted out of existence. His solar system with its nine revolving planets would be completely overcome by the onslaught of the unknown light. Earth was going to die.

* * *

"HOW'S THE WORK COMING?" ASKED FLLYK.

"Pretty good now that we are using the laser beam. We found a pocket of frozen fluorine which was unexpected and curious," replied Treswas.

"What's so strange about that? Fluorine freezes at -252 and it is now -365. Now let's get back to work. We have to get two hundred thousand tons of ice cut and shipped back home."

Ignoring the order, Fllyk said, "It's still strange for this is the first time we have hit frozen Fluorine."

"So what?" answered Treswas. "It is only some silly element containing one nucleus with nine silly electrons circling around it."

"Yeah, nine silly electrons," Fllyk quietly replied.

The laser cut deeper through the frozen fluorine pocket which had been untouched for billions of years.

The Earth died.

NUMBERS

NUMBERS LOVED MELVIN. NOT IN THE METAPHORICAL OR anthropomorphized meaning but in the literal translation of the words. Numbers loved Melvin.

His parents speculated it had something to do with his infancy. When he was given the traditional set of alphabet blocks, he was drawn to the numbers and paid little attention to the letters. He would lovingly arrange the blocks so the numbers faced up and were in order. Then he would spend hours tracing each number with the same attention a child would give to a kitten. The red 1, the blue 2, the green 3; each number had a special connection to him.

At night, when other children would cry to have their favorite stuffed bear or soft doll placed in their beds, Melvin would cry for his number blocks. After he carefully placed them in order, he would lightly caress them until sleep overcame him. Often, he would wake with the imprint of a number on his cheek or forehead, much to his glee but to his parents' dismay.

While other boys drew pictures of dinosaurs and great war battles, Melvin would fill his pages with numbers. He was the youngest of three children and once while accompanying his parents in picking up with his older brother from school, he wandered off. While exploring, he walked by an open classroom with a long multiplication problem on the chalkboard.

Melvin went to the chalkboard and stared at the numbers. Suddenly, he saw the solution appear as golden numbers below the equation. They looked like a glowing hot golden wire. This was the first time the numbers spoke to Melvin. He was unaware that, he alone, saw numbers as he did. He copied the golden answer on the board and walked away. His family stood at the doorway confused at what they'd just seen.

From that moment on, whenever Melvin saw a math problem, the answer would appear to him as golden fluorescent numbers. This was a blessing and a curse. Even though the correct answer would always take shape in his mind, he didn't have a better understanding of the mechanics of the math problem than his classmates. He would just see the solution as floating glowing objects. On tests where he was required to show his work, his grades were only average as a correct answer without the proper mechanics often was counted wrong. On standardized tests, his scores were impeccable, and he was regularly accused of cheating although a method was never discovered.

Once his unique ability was brought to public attention, he was studied and probed by the most prestigious universities and government facilities with little understanding or discernment. He was no more than a curiosity beyond any scientific explanation or comprehension. A mathematical savant. At first, he enjoyed the attention. Although, it made him feel special, he soon became bored with all the 'white coats' as he called them. For a while there was speculation he might be of use in checking important calculations relating to the space program or national defense, but it was discovered that in this area he was no better than a computer. Scientific interest in his ability soon faded.

After graduating from high school, he made a decent living hustling in Oklahoma and Arkansas casinos which allowed gambling at age 18. All digital gambling was nothing more than a series of 1's and 0's of coded software. The instant he touched a machine, the numbers who loved him would take over. Within a few years, he had been banned from all casinos and bingo halls. Anywhere gambling was controlled by computer, he was unwelcome.

He took this as a sign it was time to take his gambling proceeds and pursue a college degree. He looked for a program where his special relationship with numbers might be useful. He received his undergraduate business degree and was plodding through his MBA. It was finals week and he was studying in the library, sitting at his favorite table. He noticed a pretty brunette sitting across from him. By the look of her textbooks, she was working on a higher degree in mathematics.

He had used his ability with numbers as an ice breaker with women many times before, passing it off as a magic trick to impress the person of interest.

"Would you like me to check your work? I'm pretty good with numbers," he said with mock humility.

The young woman removed the pencil, which she was gnawing on, from her mouth and gave Melvin a long look.

"You're not in the math department," she finally replied.

"No, but I…"

"But you think you can check my work in theoretical mathematics relating classical fluid dynamics and the Navier-Stokes Equation?"

"Well, yes."

After another long pause she flipped the yellow legal pad containing several problems around and slid it over to him.

"I've got to make a phone call. Don't make any changes or go and screw things up. This is going to be good." She smirked at Melvin and left the table.

Melvin smiled to himself as this was the reaction he was accustomed to receiving. People thought he was joking with them or that he was a quack. Some might accuse him of toying with people, but it was all a part of his game.

He quickly looked over the pages that contained several long and highly evolved math problems. For the most part, her work was spot on except for two small errors involving a dropped negative sign and a numerical transposition.

When the young woman returned, she asked, "So, what did you find?" her voice dripping with sarcasm.

"Well," he said slowly for maximum effect, "for the most part, your work is solid."

"Whoa. Let's back that bus up" she interrupted with noticeable impatience. "My work is solid for the most part?"

Melvin noticed her cheeks had become flush with anger. After a well-rehearsed long pause, he said, "You dropped a negative sign on the second problem and transposed a couple of numbers on the last problem."

"You're telling me in this short time I was gone you checked all of the problems? You must be crazy."

"Yes, see for yourself." He gently slid her pad to her. "If I am wrong then I will accept the title of crazy but if I am right, then maybe you would have a cup of coffee with me?"

With a scowl, she snapped the papers back and began to check where he had indicated the mistakes were found.

He got up and asked, "Would you mind watching my stuff for second?"

Focusing on the math, and without bothering to look up, she snapped, "Yeah."

With that, he went wandering through the library to give her time to find the errors for herself. When he returned, he could tell by her countenance that she was confused and frustrated.

"So, are you some type of math wizard or what?" she asked as he sat down.

"It would be closer to the 'or what.'"

She didn't say anything. The way she looked at him brought to mind someone watching an ameba under the microscope.

"My name is Melvin," he said resting his arms on the table and leaning forward. "If you have the time, I have a story about my relationship with numbers you might find interesting."

"My name is Emily and I have some time." For the first time, she smiled. "I guess I'll take that cup of coffee.

They spent the next couple hours exploring his past and the way he saw numbers. Emily was fascinated and tried to throw him math curve balls which he batted away with ease.

Their relationship moved through the acquaintance phase, the new friendship stage, the budding romance and into the passionate lovers' endpoint. They spent many long evenings together as she tried to understand his unique ability. As for Emily, she also loved numbers and mathematics and seemed to have an uncanny ability to understand and grasp the most complex mathematical concepts.

For Emily, she was falling deeply in love with Melvin. For Melvin, this was a well scripted dalliance. He was very familiar with casual relationships and wondered if he even had the ability to experience true love.

Emily finished her doctorate in late December and was offered a research position at an out-of-state University. To celebrate, they decided to meet at a lodge in the mountains. As he drove along the snow-packed roads, he knew he was driving into inevitability. Her car was already there when he pulled into the plowed parking lot. Emily was waiting for him in the lobby as he tried to stomp the snow off of his shoes.

"Is everything okay?" She queried noticing that his embrace was stiff and lacked warmth.

"Yes, I just have a lot on my mind."

The lodge had several electronic slot machines in the bar which welcomed him with lights, bells and the sound of coins falling into metal trays. Half showing off and half to **lessen** his guilt over what was to come, he walked over to the slot machine. On the first spin he won the $1000 jackpot. He faked surprise and delight as the bar manager cashed out his winnings, which he took to the table and handed to Emily.

"This is to say congratulations on your graduation and landing your new job"

Emily looked at the money, her faced clouded with condemnation. "I can't take this. It feels like stealing."

"Okay" he replied with a shrug and put the money to one side.

The dinner was tense and filled with inconsequential small talk. Eye contact was minimal. After dinner, when the check came, numbers lit up showing him a mistake had been made. When he showed the waitress the error, she apologized profusely and brought back a corrected check. He paid for dinner and left the $1000 as a tip. Money had very little value to him.

Emily watched in silence.

They walked to the porch surrounding the lodge and watched as new snow fell. There was a crispness in the air that was common for this time of year.

"So, are you going to tell me what's been bothering you since you got here?" Emily placed her hand on his arm and was painfully aware that he tensed at her touch.

Melvin paused and let out a large sigh as if the next words were coming from a place of great anguish.

"Well, you'll be moving away as you start your new job and—"

"And you're coming with me, aren't you?"

"Uh, er. No. In fact, I thought this seemed like the right time for us to break off our relationship."

"Are you breaking up with me? But I love you," Emily said her voice cracking as tears welled in her eyes.

"I know, you're great. It's not you, it's me. I just don't feel the same way. I'm sorry" he said with feigned emotion. "The room is already paid for the next two days, so I think you should stay. I'm going back to town"

Emily sobbed. "But can't we talk about this?"

"We just did" he replied callously. Melvin turned and walked off the porch toward his car which was dusted with snow. He didn't look back.

He could still hear Emily crying with a depth that only comes from a shattered heart as he closed his car door. Driving down the winding mountain road, he was aware of the rhythmic woosh-woosh of his windshield wipers as well as the gnawing guilt in his soul.

Something was wrong. The car was speeding up, although he wasn't pushing the accelerator. The motor surged as he turned into a hairpin curve. Frantically, he pumped the brakes, but there was no response. He was going into an out of control spin and then his steering went out. At times like these, time seems to slow down and in the seconds before he crashed through the guard barrier, he thought about Emily, numbers and his mostly wasted life.

As he crashed into the rocks below, his last cognizant thought was that the check engine light had just turned on.

The next day, after Melvin's body had been removed from the carnage, the police questioned Emily about Melvin's mental state. She explained about the breakup and the officer seemed surprise that it was

Melvin who had ended the relationship. Emily pushed for an explanation and the officer remarked that the car's computer confirmed that the crash had occurred while the car was accelerating and that there were no skid marks signaling an attempt to brake. All of the cars systems seemed to have been working perfectly at the time of the crash.

Emily had no explanation and was a mixture of confused emotions.

What Melvin never knew or guessed, was that because numbers were infinite, the love that numbers could bestow was infinite as well.

It was a fact that numbers loved Melvin, but it was also a fact that numbers loved Emily more.

PRAYERS TO THE GALACTIC GOD

THE SILENCE OF THE ICU CUBICLE WAS ONLY BROKEN BY THE repetitive *click-hiss-sigh* of the ventilator. As he held the hand of his comatose daughter, he recalled how excited she had been when he told her of his new posting as Assistant Envoy to the United Council of Planets in the space colony recently established in the Therbian system. She had been so excited at the prospect of meeting and interacting with the numerous races inhabiting the space colony with the free-spirited passion found only in an 11-year-old girl. As a single parent with no real ties to his mother planet, he saw this move as a new start for his daughter and for himself.

For the first year, every day had been a new and exciting adventure. He looked forward to their evening meal when he would hear about each new discovery she'd had as she interacted with the many species attending her colony school.

Then came the morning he found her crying in her bed complaining of a severe headache. This led to a visit to the colony's hospital which eventually resulted in the words no parent would ever want to hear.

Inoperable brain tumor.

Even with all of the miraculous technologies which had brought man to the stars, there were still medical conditions humbling the pride of science for its inability to alter the natural course of the disease process.

And so, he prayed.

He prayed to his God. The one he remembered learning about as a child in a Southern Baptist Sunday school.

He prayed using the names Elohim and Adonai as was the Jewish tradition.

He prayed to Allah as it was spoken in the Qur'an.

He prayed to the gods of Hinduism.

He prayed using the 101 names of God as was described in the ancient Zoroaster texts.

He prayed to the tree gods as prescribed by the Druids.

He prayed to the Great Sand Worm worshiped by the Threkkels of Alpha Centauri B.

He sang prayer, as was custom, to the winged god of the Avian race of the planet Chriiple whose name sounded like a trill and was impossible to be pronounced by the human tongue.

He prayed to the three-faced god of the Brakeens.

He burnt incense to Hoshan, the goddess of life as dictated by the holy men of Danti' Thi.

He sacrificed a white mouse from the colony's lab to the volcanic god of the Voltarens.

He chanted sacred mantras found in the holy books of the Wvaar dating back more than 30,000 years.

He did all this and more.

And yet, his daughter died.

QUARANTINE

Xenoanthropology: Initial report

Date:5045-1-01

Senior Research Anthropologist: Xuia-nia

Subject: Anthropology studies of species 12.586.0352, system ☐434-34-☐8675., body 3

We have made initial contact with an indigenous species of this culture. They call themselves the Lakota. The hyperbolic cloaking devices as well as the Xenophonic translators are working well. We will begin the process of cultural and species studies in preparation for preliminary discussions relating to possible future admission to the Delta Union.

Personal Journal:

Date:5045-1-01

Xenoethnobiologist Class One: Zinu-naugh

This is so exciting. After all of the years of study and classroom work, I am finally in the field. We have been assigned to a planet in the □434-34-□8675 system, body 3, which has a wide variety of indigenous life. Senior anthropologist Xuia-nia has chosen a nomadic people as the initial study focus. This is a tribal society and we have identified ourselves as Shaman's from another tribe from the western mountains to explain our lack of knowledge of their local traditions. The cloaking devices are working just like they did in class. I doubt I will be able to sleep tonight. This is so great.

Xenoanthropology: Data log

Date:5045-1-31

Senior Research Anthropologist: Xuia-nia

Subject: Continuing anthropology studies of species 12.586.0352, system □434-34-□8675., body 3

We have settled into a daily routine with this tribe. Initial observations indicate a culture with strong family values based on group cooperation and sharing. These people seem to have a great respect for their environment. As Shamans, or mystical healers, we are given a respectful distance and are able to move through the camp with relative freedom. This culture seems to be rich with ceremony and tradition. Holoprojections of the traditional dances will be forwarded.

Personal Journal:

Date:5045-2-30

Xenoethnobiologist Class One: Zinu-naugh

Every day is a new adventure. Everything they need in order to exist comes from the animals and the land. Food, clothing, shelter, musical instruments, children's toys; all come from the environment. The people have learned to live in harmony with their surroundings. The children find us to be strange and exciting. They laugh at us often because of the simple things we do not know. Although we have been accepted into the tribe, they seem to think we are not very bright. I now wish I would've paid more attention during the classes on Native Weaving and Sewing, as well as Primitive Use of Skins-basic tanning.

Xenoanthropology: Data log

Date:5045-4-20

Senior Research Anthropologist: Xuia-nia

We have made a significant breakthrough with the tribe after facilitating the healing of the tribal chief's son. We have been asked to participate in the ritual Sun Dance which seems to be a very important ceremony for this indigenous culture. It should last approximately 4-8 days and seems to celebrate the balance and harmony between the stages of life and death. This culture views life/death as a circular continuum of rebirths. There is also a secondary theme running through the ceremony representing the interdependence between all of nature, including all life forms and the belief that there is a life energy or force that pervades all of creation.

I will be up loading holoprojection of a symbolic artifact given to the research party in appreciation of medical intervention on behalf of the ill child. They call this the *perjuta womime* which can be translated as a medicine wheel.

Personal Journal:

Date:5045-4-24

Xenoethnobiologist Class One: Zinu-naugh

What a great week. Senior Xuia-nia is a genius. When the son of the tribal chief became ill with a lung infection, I thought he was going to die. Senior Xuia-nia had me devise a native chant and a ritual dance involving a significant amount of smoke from a local herb. If I must say so myself, I was quite convincing as a Shaman. While the father and other members of the tribe were being distracted by my performance, Senior Xuia-nia provided a biologic inoculation. He is everything an anthropologist should be, and I count myself as lucky to be able to serve with him as colleague and student.

Xenoanthropology: Data log

Date:5046-2-20

Senior Research Anthropologist: Xuia-nia

Every day I am more impressed with the richness of this culture. Theirs is an oral history told in stories and they seem to have a story or legend to explain everything. They use these oral traditions to explain concepts such as creation and to impart knowledge, wisdom and cultural customs. A significant amount of these legends also involve local animals and fauna. The maturity of their culture leads me to consider making the recommendation for the mentoring of this race as a prelude to consideration for admission to the Delta Union.

Personal Journal:

Date:5046-7-24

Xenoethnobiologist Class One: Zinu-naugh

We are in the process of helping the tribe store food for the upcoming cycle of cold. Part of this involves drying large quantities of meat from sizable land animals called *tatanka*. These are hunted with a spring loaded projectile device, which, although very primitive, is wielded effectively by the men of this tribe. I have tried to master this device, much to the amusement of the children. The young boy that Senior Xuia-nia healed last year has become quite attached to me and I sometimes worry that he may see me uncloaked. How we would be received if we were seen in our true form? How would he respond if he knew that we were from beyond the stars? I'm excited about the prospect of this culture being groomed for Delta admission.

Xenoanthropology: Data log

Date:5048-5-03

Senior Research Anthropologist: Xuia-nia

There is a disturbance in the village. The men are gathering their weapons as the women are packing food and clothing. There is a more technological advanced culture that seems to be threatening the Lakota. The term they use for this aggressive culture can be roughly translated as *men of the long knife.* I will be up loading the recording of their phonetic and speech patterns, as well as the most up-to-date translations of the native language which we have been compiling over the past several sun cycles. The amount of fear is something we have not encountered before. I am concerned for the safety of the tribe as well as the research team. At some point we may need emergency extraction.

Personal Journal:

Date:5048-7-24

Xenoethnobiologist Class One: Zinu-naugh

Something is wrong. I smell smoke. Everyone is screaming and I can hear rapid small explosions. I must go now.

(keyed for immediate transmission)

Xenoanthropology: Data log

Date:5048-7-24

Senior Research Anthropologist: Xuia-nia

Immediate extraction requested. Under hostile attack by advanced culture. Extreme vicious cruelty. Slaughter of men, women and children. Admission status revoked. Repeat. Admission status revoked. Request immediate cultural quarantine of this planet. They are not ready for...

(Addendum note: Transmission ended at this point)

* * *

Office of US Military Telegraph

War Department

The following telegraph was received at Washington, 10 AM on December 30, 1890.

From Colonel James Forsyth, regimental commander, 7th Calvary Regiment.

While trying to disarm hostiles of Sioux nation, resistance was encountered which resulted in the deaths of 25 troopers and the wounding of 39. Approximately 150 Indians died during the altercation. The troops performed admirably and commendations will be in order. Further details to follow.

Personal Diary

Major Samuel Witside

Dakota territories, December 31, 1890

While burying the dead Sioux, we came across two abominations of nature. Two bodies were found in the burned ruins which looked to be spawned by some kind of unholy demon. They had large misshapen heads and evil dark oval-shaped eyes that are not found in nature. The arms and legs were so long and thin that I doubt they could hold up their own bodies. In the debris, we also found some burned mechanical devices which we could not identify. The men of the burial detail were quite unnerved by the discovery of these bodies. I can only assume that this is some type of deformed monstrosity as a result of heathen inbreeding. I pray that we were able to stop this infestation here.

End

LIFE SAVER

DR. DARREN MOON WAS A MAN POSSESSED. UP UNTIL FIVE years ago, his life had been headed in the right direction. He'd been a research scientist at the Jet Propulsion Laboratory, working on quantum physics relating to the study of time. He had a beautiful wife and they'd been expecting their first child.

When his wife, Julie, finally went into labor, at 41 weeks, he was so excited he could hardly contain himself. He called his wife's parents to let them know what was going on while driving to the hospital. Darren and Julie walked to the information desk and were directed to the labor and delivery unit. A nurse took his wife to a labor room while he stayed to complete the admission procedures. The young clerk couldn't help but be affected by his contagious, beaming smile. His excitement was palpable. The clerk had an opened pack of Life Savers which she offered to him. He looked at the outreached hand and noticed the top piece of candy was cherry, his favorite. He took the offered candy and impatiently waited while the clerk finished the admission process.

He joined his wife in her room. She was in early labor and wanted to walk in the halls as long as possible. They had walked to the other end of the long hospital corridor to look at the newborns in the nursery, holding hands and chatting as they gazed in awe at the many new lives before them.

A gurgling noise caught his attention, and he turned to look at his wife.

"Darren, I think something's coming out," she said.

"The baby?"

"No, something else."

She lifted up her gown to see what it could be. "Oh, my God."

Darren could see two loops of umbilical cord dangling from her vagina. He shouted for help as he laid her down on the floor. The nurses moved with great speed, but by the time they had taken his wife to the c-section room and the anesthesiologist and obstetrician had arrived, it was too late. His son was born dead. The prolapsed cord resulted in the blood supply to the baby being cut off as the head had compressed the cord.

Julie had never recovered from the loss and had withdrawn into deep spells of depression which had eventually destroyed their marriage. Since the loss of his child and wife, he'd become obsessed with his work. He worked long into the night and on weekends. Although his behavior was worrisome to his supervisors, the quality of his work was unsurpassed, so allowances were made. No one knew the reason behind the dedication driving him on year after year. He was convinced that, if the secrets of time could be discovered, he would be able to go back and change the events that had robbed him of his happiness and future.

After days of not leaving the lab, Darren finally solved the formula that allowed him to travel back and forth through time. He kept the secret to himself as he had his own plans for its use. In the locked basement of his house, he had duplicated much of the instrumentation found at the main lab. He built a prototype device and set the time to before the cord accident. His research had indicated when he returned to the past; both personalities would merge together as one being shared by two consciousnesses. It would be as if a person had two hard drives on one computer. Each consciousness would be independent, yet aware of the other.

When he manifested in the past, on the day of his child's birth he was quietly stoic. Julie had questioned him but assured her it was just new dad jitters.

Darren and his wife walked to the nurse's station of the hospital to be admitted to the labor and delivery unit. Julie was taken to a labor room and Darren stayed at the desk to complete the admission process. The young clerk could not help but notice Darren was nervous and agitated. His tension was palpable. She had an opened pack of Life Savers which she offered to him. He looked at the outreached hand and noticed the top piece of candy was cherry. He was not in the mood for candy as he knew what events were going to unfold.

When his wife wanted to walk in the halls, he refused to let her get out of bed and demanded the obstetrician be called immediately. He also demanded to speak with the anesthesiologist as well. His wife and the nurses thought he'd gone insane but to calm him down, they called the doctor and he'd come to the hospital.

This time when his wife's membranes ruptured, the emergency c-section went well due to the fact everyone was available. Several people had remarked how lucky it was he had demanded to see the physicians.

He then returned to the future, expecting everything to be different, but what he found terrified him. Ninety percent of the world's population had been destroyed by some unknown plague. He didn't know how this happened, but he knew that by changing the past, the future had also been altered. He struggled with the knowledge that saving his son had killed over six billion people. Although, tormented, he had but one option available to him.

He had to go back in time again and this time, allow his son to die.

He did this, but when he returned to the future, nothing had changed. The plague had still occurred with the same disastrous results. Somehow, he had altered the future in some way he did not understand. What detail, what action, could have been so important it altered the course of human history?

He replayed the events countless times until he discovered it was the smallest, most seemingly unimportant and random event which had changed the future to its apocalyptic conclusion. It was all about the pack of Life Savers.

In all of the previous future scenarios, he refused the ward clerks offer of the candy. He didn't realize the significance of this action. In the new, altered realities, he hadn't taken the cherry Life Saver.

Several hours later, the admissions clerk would offer a dark-haired man of Middle Eastern origin a Life Saver as well. He would look down at the cherry-flavored Life Saver and refuse it as he had a disdain for the particular flavor. The Middle Eastern man asked for directions to the research labs. He was meeting with a lab technician with his same political ideation. He would be given a newly altered genetic strain of the Ebola virus. This man, who was a genetic terrorist, would take this virus and with a few special modifications, he would create the most deadly plague the world had ever seen.

In the first reality, Darren had taken the red Life Saver and when the clerk offered a Life Saver to the dark-haired man, he would have accepted it because it was lime, his favorite flavor. He then would have choked on it and died, therefore he would have never developed the strain of plague virus. In the subsequent realities, he had refused the Life Saver.

After recreating the events of his son's birth many times, he finally discovered the proper sequence of events allowing him to save his son's life without destroying the world.

This time he took the red Life Saver.

SMALL SAVIOR

(One for the boys)

AT ABOUT 1:00 A.M., I HEARD A THUMP I THOUGHT CAME
from the roof. I'd just gone to bed and I wasn't sure if I'd been dreaming. It
was a windy night in November and my wife, Liz, had gone to Dallas to do
some shopping while I was home alone with my two boys, Lawrence and
Matthew, ages 12 and 9.

The next morning, I noticed the faint odor of burning wood as I
started down the stairs. We lived in a two-story house with a castle turret
leading to the upstairs landing. I figured someone in the neighborhood was
using their fireplace – a common practice this time of year. Matthew and
Lawrence were downstairs, planted in front of the TV set on the kitchen
island. This was their favorite place to eat breakfast.

"Are you guys cooking anything?" I asked,

"No, Dad. We're just eating cereal."

Putting the odor out of my mind, I went back upstairs to work on my computer.

Suddenly I felt pain shoot through the little toe on my right foot. "Lawrence," I shouted, "Your ferret is out again and is attacking me!"

Lawrence came running up the stairs and picked up a small gray ferret busy nipping at my feet. "Oh, Dad, you know Friskie really likes you. It's his way of asking for a piece of apple as a snack."

"That is a killer ferret who needs to be made into a small rug," I retorted. Though I'd tried to develop a relationship with this small fur ball, it seemed I was the one it liked to attack. I took it personally, but Lawrence thought it was funny.

"Take the ferret away and put it back it its cage. Fix that latch." The latch was loose and Friskie could work it open with some effort. I'd been on Lawrence for weeks to fix it, but he had an affinity with the 'P' word: procrastination.

"And don't you have some homework to do?" I called after him as he was leaving the room. Homework was one of those subjects Matthew, Lawrence, and I spent a lot of our time either fighting about, avoiding, or sometimes, even, doing. I wasn't working that weekend and we had planned to veg out in front of the TV watching a stack of rented movies.

Suddenly I heard Matthew call out, "Dad, we don't have any water."

Darn it, I thought. They were building a house on the empty lot next to ours and this wouldn't have been the first time workers had cut one of the lines.

I got up from the computer and went to the phone to call the water department, noticing the house was getting very cold – odd, as the furnace was new. I wondered if they'd gotten the gas lines too. I picked up the receiver and heard no dial tone. "Crap," I muttered under my breath as I went downstairs to check the other phones. All of them were dead.

Matthew was on my heels. "Dad, it's really getting cold in here. Why isn't there any heat?"

"I don't know," I answered trying to manage my temper, but inside I was furious at some incompetent worker who was messing up my Saturday. "Let's go up to the attic and check out the system."

"I want to come, too," quipped Lawrence, who never wanted to be left out of anything. The boys bounded up the stairs leading to the turret, competing to see who would be first and fighting all the way up the stairs.

"Guys, stop it!" I yelled. "We don't need fighting on top of everything else going on today."

"Dad, look, there's a hole in the door!" cried Matthew.

As I entered the landing I was thinking, *What else can go wrong?* Lawrence and Matthew were staring through a hole in the base of the solid wood door leading to the turret. "Get out of the way, guys. Let me see what's going on."

I knelt at the door to look at the hole and noticed the faint smell of burning wood I had noticed before. The hole was about ten inches high and five inches wide and was cut out of the door with surgical precision. A weird feeling tingled in my gut, and an electric shock went down my spine. I got down on my knees and noticed no air was coming through the hole. I couldn't feel the cold I expected to be blowing in. I peered through the hole and noticed a haze I couldn't quite see through. Through the distortion, there appeared to be some type of dark object sitting on the turret. I got up from my knees and tried to open the door. It didn't budge. It wasn't like it was locked because there was no movement of the handle. There was no give in the door at all. It was as if the door was solid block of granite weighing thousands of pounds.

"Dad, what's wrong?" Lawrence asked, his voice tinged with fear.

"Yeah, what's wrong?" Matthew also chimed, moving closer to my side as if to get away from some unknown fear.

"I don't know. I don't know," I said, trying to be calm, but knowing they could hear the worry in my voice. I got back down on my knees and tried to put my hand through the opening, but was stopped by an invisible force feeling as immovable as the door. Now I was scared. My sci-fi loving brain knew there was something abnormal going on. Something dangerous.

"Get down the stairs now," I ordered to the boys.

"Why, Dad? What's wrong?"

"Don't argue. Just get down the stairs. Now!" My tone brought immediate silence as they started down the stairs. Silence was not like them. It made me realize they were scared and knew something was terribly wrong.

As we reached the bottom of the stairs, the electricity went off in the house.

I could hear the terror in Matthew's voice, as he whispered, "Dad."

"Let's get out of the house. Everyone go to the garage and get into the car. Now!"

For once there were no arguments, no questions. We all piled into the Lexus in a frantic dash. I fumbled with my keys and got them into the ignition, but when I turned the key, nothing happened. The car was dead.

"I'm scared," Matthew said with a trembling voice.

"Me too," Lawrence echoed. Their eyes were wide, glistening and rimmed with tears.

"Everything is going to be all right," I tried to reassure them. I attempted using the cell phone, but it was also dead. "Come on, guys. Let's go out the front door."

We all fell out of the car, ran back into the house and headed to the front door only to find it was stuck solid just like the turret door. We then ran to the back door, but it too was fixed as an immovable mass. In a fit of dramatic desperation, I picked up a solid brass duck from the coffee table and hurled it at the patio door. It bounced off with a loud thud and fell to the floor. We all looked at each other, realizing we were trapped in our house. Then a noise echoed down from upstairs in the attic and I saw the boys shiver as they realized something was in the house with us.

"Boys, go to the solarium."

I started up the stairs to go to the bedroom closet where I kept the guns. I heard Lawrence behind me yelling "Friskie, Dad! Don't forget Friskie!" I could hear strange scraping sounds from the turret stairway. There was light coming in from the bedroom skylight, and I felt in the shadows for the 12-gauge. Trying to steady my shaking hands, I hurriedly grabbed a box of slugs and headed down the stairs. *The ferret*, I thought. I turned and looked in Lawrence's room and saw the cage was empty. Deciding it might be too dangerous to waste time looking for the rodent, I moved on.

When I reached the solarium my boys were huddled in the far corner. I closed the door and locked it. I then placed the hot tub steps and the plant stand in front of the door. In my heart I knew we were up against some alien force unlikely to be slowed by my futile and petty attempts at defense. But, somehow it made me feel better. As I loaded the shotgun, I finally had time to think. Was this some alien attack, or was it something from *Poltergeist* with supernatural malevolent involvement? I loved to read science fiction, and it was easy for me to think in logical terms about the most illogical scenarios. I believed in extra-terrestrial life and considered the possibility we had been invaded or attacked by some cosmic force. I remembered seeing something on the turret through the mist. Could it have been an alien spaceship or probe? I considered a probe more likely because of the small size of the ship. But who said aliens had to be my size? What if it was something out of *Gulliver's Travels* where he met the Lilliputians. The hole in the door had definitely been cut by some type of laser or energy tool. What other weapons could they have? Why were they here? The fact they had trapped us inside our house implied they had plans for us. What these plans could be only made me shudder.

"What's happening?" Matthew asked.

"I don't know, but I think we've been trapped in the house by some-thing alien."

"Like the *X-files*?" Lawrence asked.

"Yes, but this is for real. Something has cut off our electricity, water, and phone system. It must be sending out some kind of dampening field draining the car and not letting the car phone work."

"But Dad, this can't be happening. All that stuff just happens on TV, and you always told us that it wasn't real."

"I know. I know. I don't understand it but we can't ignore the facts. How else would you explain what's happened today?"

Lawrence noticed his ferret wasn't with us. "Dad, you forgot Friskie!" he cried.

"I didn't forget him. He got out of his cage again and he was gone when I went for him."

"Friskie, *Friskie*!" he called.

"Lawrence, we are not going to open the door and look for him. I'm sure he's okay."

We sat in the afternoon light of the solarium, quiet, almost afraid to speak for what seemed like hours. I couldn't help but wonder what was going through the boys' minds. Were they thinking about their mother? Were they old enough to think about dying? Were they envisioning them-selves being transported to some far away planet?

"Get in the hot tub. I'm going to shoot the patio door and see if we can break through this force field." I didn't know if the bullet would rico-chet, and I figured the tub with the water would be the safest place. They hurriedly climbed into the tub and, for once, Matthew didn't complain about the water being too hot.

"When I count to three take a deep breath and go under the water. Ready? One, two, three." When I heard them slosh in the water, I fired the slug into the patio glass. The sound was deafening in the closed room. There, on the floor, the slug was flattened out.

"Dad, what are we going to do now?" asked Lawrence with a ragged breath as he came up for air.

"I don't know, but I think it's time we pray." As we held each other closely, me reciting the Lord's Prayer, the boys shivered, both from fear and their wet clothes.

A sound from overhead in the attic reverberated throughout the room. It was a high pitch squeal and a crash as if someone had dropped several kitchen pans.

"What was that?" my sons asked in unison.

"It sounds like they're building something."

We crouched farther back into the corner away from the door. After several hours of what seemed like an eternity, the lights suddenly came on. We rushed to the patio door leading outside. The handle turned easily. We ran into the afternoon chill, into the freedom of the front yard. It was about four in afternoon, daylight waning, as we ran across the street and stared back at the house that had been our cage.

"Dad, look." Matthew was pointing up to the castle turret. We could feel a low vibration and heard mechanical humming. A small object hovered in the air over the turret for a second before shooting up into the sky and out of sight. Later, we argued about the shape. I thought it was box-like, but the boys thought it was more of a cigar shape, but no one doubted its existence.

"You wait here while I go check things out. I think whatever it was is gone," I said.

"Don't leave us!" The boys were stuck to me like glue.

With caution, we went back into the house. I held the shot gun out in front of me with the safety off. We opened the front door. Nothing happened. We entered the foyer and noticed the heat was back on, and I could hear the sound of running water in the sink which Matthew had turned on what seemed like days ago.

As we turned the corner to head up the stairs, I saw something coming down towards us. "Get back!" I yelled as I raised the gun to fire.

"Stop, Dad! It's Friskie!" Lawrence exclaimed as he reached for his ferret, whose left ear had been burned off and one of his teeth missing. He had a long cut along his hip and he was limping.

We never knew what had happened that day, but it was obvious the little ferret had tangled with our unwelcome guests. We wondered how the other guy looked. All I could assume was, whatever had taken over the house had not planned on defending itself from a furry ball of fight.

When my wife returned home, we tried to explain what had happened but even with the burned hole in the door, I don't think she ever really believed us. Still, we knew the truth. We knew what had happened.

I still don't like the ferret, but I don't make jokes about turning him into a small fur rug anymore. And sometimes when the boys aren't looking, I sneak him a small bit of apple.

TAU CETI

THE SIX OFFICERS OF THE *EXPLORER 14* CROWDED ONTO THE
command deck as their long awaited prize came into view. They were
oblivious to the low hum of their AI drone hovering behind them. Even
with the invention of the Q-Drive, the trip still took over seven months to
arrive at Tau Ceti. By observing wobbles in the parent star, five planets were
identified in 2012 by ancient telescopes. There was significant excitement
when research probes had returned identifying two planets existing in the
temperate sweet zone for possible habitation. P4 was seen as having the
most promising environment which was the cause of the excitement and
anticipation as they settled into stationary orbit.

"Rey, what do you think?" Captain Alan Harkin asked his sci-
tech officer.

Reyansh Patel was a seasoned science and technical officer and even
though this was his fourth exploratory mission, Alan thought he could hear
a bit of excitement in his voice. "The scans are showing an atmosphere that

is within two percent of Earth's 21/78 ratio of oxygen/nitrogen. The oxygen is at 19% so it will be breathable if we can clear it for toxins," replied Rey.

"Toxins?" The question came from the *Explorer 14*'s second, Mei Zhu. She was the youngest of the crew and although she had with been on several interstellar missions, this was her first FC mission.

"Yes, this is not like a holo-vid where everyone shuttles down to a first contact (FC) planet with their haz helmets off. We have to run tests to look for viruses, spores, bacteria, parasites, poisonous gases and about a thousand other nasty things that can kill you…. and us for that matter," answered Rey in his best professorial voice.

Harkin added, "Yes, we will be collecting and sifting through data for several weeks before we make planetfall. Alfred, what do you know so far?"

Alfred was the name given to one of *Explorers 14* three AI drones. Each mission vessel was equipped with three AI drones and the other two were in storage but they were continuously synched to Alfred so that if Alfred was ever damaged or destroyed, the next AI drone could take over with a seamless transition. Harkin had always thought that Alfred looked like a large black checker that was always hovering in the background except when charging in its power dock.

"Captain, initial scans indicate two large land masses comprising thirty percent of the planet's surface area. The poles are covered ice similar to Earth's and the temperature at the equator averages 20°C. There seem to be numerous lakes and rivers with three dominant mountain ranges. This is the most earth-like planet that has yet to be discovered by any of the numerous exoplanet missions," replied Alfred.

Alfred was programmed with an endless number of voices ranging from sexy and seductive to robotic and mechanical. Harkin, along with most of his fellow Navy cadets, had spent many hours watching all of the old TV shows that had depicted what early writers speculated the future of space travel would be like. The cadets had found it fascinating to see what early Earth writers had gotten right about the future and how many things that they had missed the mark on. His favorite archived series was *Star Trek*. Therefore out of deference, he had programmed Alfred to sound like the original but ancient science officer Spock.

* * *

A WEEK LATER, AT THEIR DAILY SUMMATION MEETING, THE crew was going over the most recent scans.

"Rey, can you bring us up to date of where we stand at this point?" asked Harkin. Except for the captain, the crew seldom used formal title ranks during routine conversations.

"Yes, Captain." Rey paused as he looked over his data feeds. "Every day, it keeps getting better and better. Geologically, the planet is relatively stable. The axis of the planet indicates that there are no wide temperature fluctuations. The biological scans do not show any large predators and most of the larger life forms are either omnivores or herbivores. The air, soil and water samples have yet to show any pathogens or toxins. I am not saying that this planet is the Garden of Eden but it sure is in the running for that designation." He paused to let them grasp implication of his words.

"So, what are we waiting for?" quipped Mei.

"I know you're all itching to step foot on a brand-new planet but that planet isn't going anywhere and neither are we. We did not come 12 light years to get sloppy now. Alfred, what do you think?"

"I agree with Lieutenant Patels assessment. The data from the scans and the probes are all within normal parameters. Although…" Alfred paused at this point which was something unexpected from an artificial intelligent construct.

"Alfred?" Captain Harkin always envisioned the iconic pointed ear Vulcan when talking to Alfred. Harkin thought he could almost hear Alfred's processors working.

"There seems to be some high energy readings coming from the far side of the planet that do not readily conform to any known energy spectrum. They come and go with no identifiable pattern," answered Alfred.

"Is it dangerous?"

"At this point, it is impossible to determine but I would suggest that we moved our orbit coordinates over the anomalies' to get a better visualization," Alfred said in his best Vulcan representation.

"Mei, lets head over to the other side and see what's concerning Alfred,"

"Aye, aye, Captain," and with that she put the new synchronization coordinated into the helm's computer that would bring the *Explore 14* into orbit over the unusual energy reading*s*.

* * *

AN HOUR LATER THEY ARRIVED OVER THE AREA WHERE THE probes had registered the anomalies. They were over the largest of the two land masses where the coast line was flush with tall bamboo like trees if the bamboo was sixty feet tall and three feet in diameter. There were long beaches with sand the color of rose quartz and gentle waves massaging the coast line.

"Will the atmosphere support a vid-drone?" asked Harkin to both his senior staff.

Alfred answered first. "Yes, Captain, the density of the atmosphere is well within the parameters that will sustain vid-drone flight."

Rey caught the eye of Mei and the look that passed between them showed their displeasure at Alfred answering for the both of them. Although the AI was supposed to lack feeling, it sometimes felt as if he was purposely trying to sabotage his human counterparts.

"Fine, then let's send down a vid-drone to get a look at whatever's causing the anomalies," ordered the captain.

Rey scowled as he looked at the data displays in front of him.

"Captain, we are getting better short-range data scans due to our closer proximity but they still do not make any logical sense."

"Tell me what you see," requested Harkin.

"Well," Rey said and hesitated. "The readings keep fluctuating between some type of unknown energy and an organic life form. And, at first, the movement seemed to be random and sporadic but when I ran the movement sequences through a pattern recognition program it showed that they most closely resemble patterns like those related to acrobatic flight maneuvers."

"Flight maneuvers? Like things we learned in basic flight training at the Academy?" asked the captain?

"Yes," answered Rey. "The patterns are similar to the slow roll, the point roll, the inverted spin and the pinwheel. Aerobatics that a pilot might perform with an aircraft."

"It couldn't just be random variations or artifact?" asked the captain after a short pause.

"I do not think so, Captain. They seem to be deliberate and controlled and they always occur when the anomaly is in its organic form."

When the capsule containing the vid-drone completed its entry into the atmosphere, a parachute deployed, slowing the capsule to allow the drone's release.

On the command deck, the senior officers studied the live video feed as it was projected across several viewing monitors.

"Let's see if we can get a closer look at the anomaly," requested the captain.

"Yes sir," replied Rey. "I will get eyeball to eyeball with this thing."

With a few keystrokes, the vid-drone started to approach the anomaly and as it advanced on the unidentified object, the object started to speed up.

"Don't let that thing get away," urged the captain.

"Yes, Captain," and with that Rey adjusted the drone's speed. Rey struggled to keep up with the anomaly as it made a series of complicated aerobatic maneuvers. "I am placing the drone on auto follow."

All eyes were on the video stream as the drone attempted to pace the anomaly as it performed barrel rolls, inverted loops and pinwheels.

"Sir, the drone is maxing out at 750 kmh. It is starting to overheat."

The anomaly suddenly stopped in midair as the vid-drone lost power and slowly descended to the beach. The anomaly landed nearby and walked over to the vid-drone, staring at the camera with one glassy black eye, its head tilted to one side.

On the bridge of the *Explorer 14*, Captain Alan Harkin was sure he heard a voice in is head.

Mei hesitantly asked, "Did anyone else hear that?"

Rey nodded yes as did several other crewmembers.

"I also received a message as if someone hacked my programming which is impossible," interjected Alfred. "Captain, what message did you receive?"

"That was fun," answered the Harkin.

All of the command deck crew murmured an agreement as they looked at each other with a combination of concern and disbelief.

Rey broke the tension with his interjection. "Sir, I have a cleaned up video feed from the drone after it landed."

"Put it up," commanded Harkin.

The video showed a picture of a clean, rose-colored beach and after a few seconds, an object landed in the cameras range and hopped towards the drone as it tilted its head to look into the camera lens. There was no doubt about what they were looking at. The anomaly looked to be an earth seagull.

"All senior staff to the ready room," snapped Harkin as he stood up, leaving the bridge.

After all the senior staff assembled with urgency, he turned to face them and said, "What the hell was that?"

"According to my database, the anomaly or creature that we saw was, or was made to resemble, the earth avian *Larus occidentalis* or the western gull that nearly went extinct during the time of the Great Pollution which lasted from 2044-2075 after which all Earth's governments banded together to reclaim the biosphere," informed Alfred.

The last member of the senior staff to reach the ready room was Chief Xenobiologist Holly Mann. Dr. Mann was from the European equivalent of NASA. She was of average build, short brown hair and delightful lilting English accent.

"Sir," Holly interjected, "I am concerned that what we are dealing with could be some type of alien being that has the ability of telepathy. If it can place words into our brains then possibly we are seeing a projection of what the alien wants us to see. I think we can all agree that an earth seagull is not 12 million light years from home. Why it decided to project itself as a seagull is only speculation unless it wanted to present itself in a non-threatening form."

"Other thoughts?" asked Captain Harkin.

"Although we have discovered numerous types of lower alien life forms, we have never encountered any species we would consider intelligent and certainly nothing approaching telepathic powers. We, therefore, have no historical basis for how we should proceed, although I think extreme caution would be warranted," said Alfred.

Harkin was always amazed how hearing the voice of Mr. Spock coming from the speaker of his AI had a calming effect on his staff.

"To me," Mei said, "The voice I heard seemed playful. I did not sense anything that caused me concern. I thought it sounded like an invitation and I think we should send a research team down to the surface. That is the only way we will know who or what we are dealing with."

Captain Harkin leaned back in his chair stared overhead for several moments.

"I agree," replied the captain. "I will take a shuttle down with Rey and Molly. Mei and Alfred, you two will monitor our video and auditory feeds as well as our scanners which we'll take down to the surface. Rey, you take the standard first landfall scanner and Molly you take your souped-up medical scanner to see what kind of creature or being we're dealing with and also to observe our brain wave activity for any type of anomaly or interference. Side arms are required"

* * *

OVER THE ROAR OF THE SHUTTLE'S ENGINES HARKIN shouted, "We will go planet side in full protective gear including helmets."

"Roger that," Molly and Rey said in unison.

They set the shuttle down about 50 meters from the anomaly life form and dropped the loading dock platform. After leaving the shuttle, they walked toward the oddity slowly with the captain in the lead and stopped within four meters of what looked like a normal Earth seagull.

"What do the scans say?" asked Harkin.

Rey answered, "I'm still reading normal atmosphere. Breathable."

"Holly?"

"Captain, if I can believe my readings, I am scanning a normal Earth western seagull."

"Could we all be experiencing some form of mass hallucination?" asked the captain, never taking his eyes off of the object identified as a seagull. And the seagull never took its black glassy eyes off of the captain.

Before anyone could answer, the seagull suddenly began to preen its feathers. It plucked one of its feathers, hopped towards Holly and dropped it a meter from her and then backed away. Holly looked at the feather and then at the captain, before bending over to pick it up. She stared at it for a moment turning it over in her hand and then she placed it in the DNA reader that was part of her medical scanner. After a minute she turned to the captain.

"It's reading normal DNA for the western gull."

Over his suit com he heard Alfred say, "Captain, I agree with Lieutenant Mann's assessment although I cannot discern any logical or rational explanation."

Harkin turned toward the entity and took a step forward. As he spoke, he also tried to form the words in his mind. "My name is Harkin. We come from another world that is very far from this one."

I know, were the words that formed in his own mind.

"Did you both get that?" he asked.

"I heard the words 'I know'" answered Holly.

"Agreed," Rey replied.

The captain continued, "What is your name? What do we call you?"

Jonathan Livingston Seagull was the reply in his mind.

"Are you folks up there getting all this?" asked the captain.

Mei quickly responded, "Yes, sir, the entire crew, as well as Alfred, are receiving the same telepathic messages.

"Does it make any sense to anyone? Does anyone have any ideas about this?" queried the captain.

No one said a thing until Alfred spoke.

"Captain, I have been searching the ancient data banks and found a reference for the name Jonathan Livingston Seagull that is approximately 410 years old. Apparently, there was a book with that title that was published in 1970 when everything was still printed on paper."

"Do you think it has any relevance?" asked Harkin.

"I did not think so until I scanned the book in its entirety. There are certain passages that, on the surface, seem to directly relate to the events we are experiencing. I will send the key passages to your video feed so you can read them and decide for yourself how to proceed."

"First, just give me a summary of the book," requested the captain.

"Yes, Sir. The story portrays the life of a seagull that is trying to achieve a Zen-like perfection through flight. As it reaches a higher spiritual state, it develops telepathy as well as time space travel."

"What do you mean 'time space travel'?" replied Harkin.

"According to the author, this seagull developed the ability to alter its physical energy state so that it could move back and forth through time as well as across interstellar space in the time it takes to process a thought," answered Alfred. "I'm sending you key passages of the book to explain."

Several lines from the book started scrolling across all the monitors of the ship as well as the viewfinders of the planet crew.

Page 53: *"Where is everybody, Sullivan?" he asked silently, quite at home now with the easy telepathy that these gulls used instead of screes and gracks.*

Page 59: *Then one day Jonathan, standing on the shore, closing his eyes, concentrating, all in a flash knew what Chiang had been telling him. "Why, that's true! I am a perfect, unlimited gull!" He felt a great shock of joy. "Good!" said Chiang, and there was victory in his voice. Jonathan opened his eyes. He stood alone with the Elder on a totally different seashore — trees down to the water's edge, twin yellow suns turning overhead. Jonathan was stunned. "Where are we?" Utterly unimpressed with the strange surroundings, the Elder brushed the question aside. "We're on some planet, obviously, with a green sky and a double star for a sun."*

Harkin, as well as most members of the crew, was having a hard time wrapping his mind around the concepts with which they were being presented. If the research that Alfred had obtained was correct, they were being asked to believe that they were in contact with an Earth seagull that had the ability to transport its physical being over 11 light years and over the time span of 400 years.

"There has got to be some other explanation. Some explanation that's more logical and reasonable and doesn't break all of the known laws of physics," stated Harkin.

"Captain, I am only reporting the data that I have received from the early Earth archives. I cannot attest to its validity although events that are unfolding seem to coincide with the author's tale," responded Alfred.

The Captain returned his gaze to the seagull that had not moved and kept tilting his head from one side to the other.

"Are you the same Jonathan Livingston Seagull that is written about in the book over 400 years ago?" asked Harkin.

"*Yep, that would be me,*" replied the bird telepathically. "*And I've been waiting for you out here for a long time.*"

Cautiously, Harkin asked, "Explain." And then after a pause, "Please."

"*For reasons that no one truly understands, some of my flock discovered that the achievement of pure flight led to the achievement of pure thought and pure thought allowed a being to convert mass into energy which was then able to transcend time and space. Unfortunately, as birds, we were only able to use this ability to travel through time and space. Without an opposable thumb, we lacked the ability to build even the simplest birdhouse. So I decided that I would pass this knowledge onto man when man was ready.*"

"How did you decide that man—that we were ready?" asked the captain.

"*You found me, didn't you? Now...one other thing.*"

"Yes?" responded Harkin. He kneeled down on the rose colored sand so that he was almost eye level with Jonathan.

"Do you have any fish?"

TEXT FROM GOD

"THIS IS THE MORNING EDITION WITH NPR RADIO," SAID HOST Steve Inskeep.

David Miller opened his eyes and tried to focus. The radio had awakened him with the familiar station; the spokesperson was discussing the latest news out of Washington. He forced himself up into a sitting position, stretched, and scratched himself a couple of times before reaching for his glasses on his nightstand. It was early, just turning light. He looked over to the other side of his king size bed which was undisturbed. Sleeping in one position so that the opposite side of the bed was undisturbed was his habit.

He pulled himself out of bed and turned of the radio off before, heading towards the bathroom. Once in the bathroom, he turned on the stereo system on the bathroom counter to continue with the Morning Edition.

It was Monday morning so he had no surgeries or elective C-sections. He'd long made it a rule to never schedule surgery on Monday mornings as history had taught him there was a very good chance he would forget about the surgery, and he hated getting a phone call stating the patient had already been seen by the anesthesiologist and the OR crew was waiting for him. He hated starting mornings in a frantic rush.

NPR radio played in the background while he showered, shaved, and completed his morning routine. After dressing, he walked back into the bedroom looking at the undisturbed side of the bed. The scene and heavy heart reminded him of one failed marriage and two empty relationships.

At 38, David was a successful OB/GYN physician in Oklahoma City with a thriving practice, a nice home, and a few good friends. But an empty bed. As he began to load up his pants with wallet, keys, and change, he reached for his pager and thought about an article he'd read which reported that physicians were the first group to start using pagers and they were now the last group to stop using them. He remembered the first time he'd been given a pager. It was when he was a medical student. For a few brief moments, the pager gave him a sense of importance, until he realized it was only a chain that could be tugged whenever someone in the world wanted him.

Only recently had he broken down, succumbed to the peer pressure of his colleagues, and purchased an iPhone. The hospital strongly suggested OB/GYN's purchase the iPhone since there was an application that allowed them to view a fetal monitor strip from their phones. It was thought that this might decrease the risk of lawsuits, which are prevalent in his field. Patients were surprised when they discovered that their doctor was not in the hospital for the duration of their labor.

Heading out to the garage, he picked his cell phone up from its standard spot in the charging dock downstairs. His calendar showed he had nothing scheduled this morning other than making hospital rounds, then going to the office for his morning appointments. He had one patient to see in the hospital, Mrs. Hightower, a sweet elderly woman from Woodward, Oklahoma who'd been referred to him for the treatment of dysfunctional uterine bleeding caused by a large uterine fibroid. Surgery had gone well on Friday and he hadn't received any calls regarding complications. He felt sure that she would be going home this morning.

He looked at the text message icon on the phone and noticed there was one unread message. *Strange,* he thought. *It must be a mistake.* Texting wasn't something he did and in fact, this was probably the first text he had ever received. The message simply read, "Take May Avenue". He looked at the top of the screen to see who had sent the message. **I AM** was the only identification showing.

It must be a mistake or a prank. He pocketed the phone as he headed to the car in the garage. He drove towards Lake Hefner Parkway, the fastest and most direct route to the hospital, a mere seven miles from his home. About a mile down the road, he came to a stop. The traffic was at a standstill, leaving him caught between exits, with no way out of the morass of cars. On the radio, he heard the report discussing an overturned 18-wheeler blocking the road ahead of him.

His jaw tightened as his frustration began to burn. He was trapped with no way out until the wreck was cleared. He was about to call the office to let them know he might be late, when an unfamiliar sound notified him of a new text message.

"I told you to take May Avenue".

He quickly looked around searching. The feeling that he must be on one of those reality shows crossed his mind.

His car was in the outside lane of the highway with a milk tanker truck to the right of him, a red Volkswagen beetle in front of him and an obviously frustrated mother with two children in the minivan behind him that he could observe in his rearview mirror. He couldn't see a hidden camera truck or van. Looking at the text message again, he decided to respond. It wasn't as if he'd be moving any time soon. "Who is this?" He paused and then touched the SEND button and with a swooping sound, his question was sent.

Quickly, rather too quickly he thought, the reply returned.

"I AM."

What the hell does that mean? He placed his phone into the cup holder built into his car's console and glanced to the right at the milk truck, and then watched the frustrated mother as she tried to break up a fight between her two children. He listened to the radio and tried to calm the tension that he could feel rising in his gut. He called labor and delivery and explained his entrapment, letting them know that if anyone came in with a precipitous labor, they would have to call one of his partners.

I AM, he thought. A flicker of a faint childhood memory began to emerge. Throughout his youth, until he'd left for college, he regularly attended a Southern Baptist Church with his family. Much to his mother's heartbreak, he never returned to the church. Every so often, he would go to an Easter or a Christmas service with his family, but he never found the comfort nor the answers in religion that others seemed to find.

He had a faint memory of "I AM" being related to some Bible story. Picking up his phone, he typed in the question "who is I AM?" into Google. Almost immediately, Wikipedia popped up. He read that in Exodus, 3:14, when Moses met God for the first time he asked for the name of God. The response was Ehyeh Asher Ehyer, commonly translated into I AM.

He almost laughed aloud at the thought that God would be texting him.

"Whatever," he replied and hit send. He waited for the response for several seconds. A smile had taken over his face at the absurdity of the idea that God would text him, when he was signaled that another text had come through. "Get ready, you're moving." He looked up in time to notice the traffic was now, once again, beginning to move and a chill ran down his spine.

* * *

THE REST OF HIS DAY WAS UNEVENTFUL, A FULL DAY OF clinic, numerous phone calls and no one in labor. He'd almost forgotten about the earlier text from I AM as he headed home to a dinner that would consist of either delivered pizza or Chinese food.

After arriving home, he placed his phone on the counter where he left it charging and he walked into the kitchen to enjoy the one beer he'd allow himself as he never knew when a patient in labor might arrive. He was old-school, meaning he went in for most of his own deliveries even though there was a group of physicians who shared evening call to whom he could delegate the delivery if he desired. He prided himself on the fact that he consistently delivered over 95% of his patients. It gave him a loyal following among his patients, but a lifestyle that left little room for friends or family. He always promised he would slow down some day, but that day never seemed to come.

As he took his first drink of a cold beer, he heard the ping of an incoming text. With slight hesitation, he got his iPhone and read the new message: "Tomorrow order 12 units of blood."

Order 12 units of blood? What the hell did that mean? He remembered that he had a repeat C-section for Tuesday morning. "Who is this?" he once again sent. "I AM" once again was the reply. He was getting angry now. Someone, who obviously knew he was a doctor and had surgery in the morning, had found his cell number and was texting him crank messages.

"So, this is God?" he replied, then waited. There was no response. He thought for a moment and then sent the second question. "If you are God, prove it." This left him feeling somewhat ridiculous. Asking for proof from the conceptual being he was not even sure he still believed in.

"Sadly, that is what you all want, and sometimes need," came the reply.

What kind of vague, bullshit answer was that?.

No sooner had he lifted his beer when another message came in. "I forgave you for killing the robin." This stopped him in mid-action, and he slowly put down his beer. He sat down at the kitchen table as he suddenly was not feeling very well.

When he was about 10 years old, he spent his summer with his grandmother who had a small five-acre farm in Choctaw, Oklahoma. He'd received a brand new Daisy BB gun for his birthday and he was out in the woods shooting at cans, bottles, and birds. He had never hit a bird and doubted that he could really hurt it because of their thick covering of feathers. He had come upon a robin who was sitting on her nest and therefore she resisted the natural urge to flee as he approached. Without thinking, he raised his BB gun, aimed, and fired. He was surprised when the bird fell from the tree, dead. In a tragic fluke, the BB pellet hat hit the robin in the head causing it to die instantly.

He had picked up the lifeless bird. Its body was limp in his hand, but still warm. A wave of grief, shame, and regret had flowed over him. He remembered burying the bird as tears cut through the red Oklahoma dust on his cheeks. He had begged God to forgive him for his thoughtless act, and he always wondered if God had heard his prayer.

He looked at the text again. "I forgave you for killing the robin." Deep shame had kept him from telling anyone. Not his parents, his best friend, nor his ex-wife. He carried this painful memory for all these years knowing that he alone knew of the dark event. That is only he, and, in theory, *God* knew.

His mind was spinning with the impossible speculation that:

1. There was a God and,

2. God would communicate with him by text.

It seemed too improbable even to conceive. He considered himself to be a rational man and although he had seen many things over his years of medicine that some would consider as miracles, he still looked to the rationality of science for most of his answers. There were no further texts and the rest of the evening was spent in conflict between the rational mind of the physician and the trusting mind of a child who once believed in the God who would forgive him for his sins.

He considered other scenarios to explained recent events. Elaborate pranks, hidden camera reality show, complicated magic tricks such as Copperfield making the Statue of Liberty disappear. None of them were adequate. Occam's Razor taught when looking for answers, bet on the one that requires the fewest assumptions, no matter how unlikely.

He had a very restless night as the events of the day kept turning over and over in his mind. The next morning, feeling somewhat foolish, he called the blood bank and ordered twelve units of blood to be typed and crossed for Mrs. Ortega. This would be Mrs. Ortega's third repeat C-section. Although repeat C-sections did increase the risk of bleeding complications to a minor extent, he'd never seen such a disaster in his practice.

The patient and her family were talked with to answer any last-minute questions. Reassurance was given them that everything would be fine. The anesthesiologist approached him and questioned why he had ordered twelve units of blood and asked if he was expecting any problems. Lying, he told him that he only had a suspicious feeling about this surgery.

The surgery started normally enough. Cutting through skin, fatty tissues, fascia and peritoneum, then the placement of a self-retaining retractor to stabilize and hold the incision open. At that point, he saw the purplish mass on the uterus indicating that there was the placenta accreta. This was the rare complication where the placenta had grown through the wall of the uterus. Without hesitation, he opened up the uterus, delivered the crying male infant, and handed the baby off to the nurses.

He then turned his attention to the hemorrhage before him. At term, the blood supply to the uterus is 500 cc, a minute. The blood loss is more than most people can comprehend. The anesthesiologist saw the bleeding and started a second line. Because of his earlier order for twelve units of blood, the anesthesiologist had already started the second line in anticipation of possible problems in the delivery. Using several surgical techniques and with help from his partner, who was called in to assist him, he finally got the uterine bleeding under control. The uterus was saved. Overall the patient did well.

At the end of the case, when he questioned the anesthesiologist about the blood loss, he was informed that the blood loss was over 5000 cc and they had used all of the twelve units of blood. The anesthesiologist remarked how lucky they were to have the blood on hand and that the outcome may have been completely different if they'd had to wait for the blood bank to bring up the required amount of replacement blood. Once again, the anesthesiologist asked Dr. Miller how he knew to order twelve units of blood. Once again, Dr. Miller lied and said that he'd just had a hunch.

He ran the day's events over and over as he drove home from work that evening. Although his rational mind was having a hard time accepting it, there was no denying that something of the supernatural was at play. This couldn't be a joke or some elaborate prank. Some force knew about his unspoken past and could predict a, supposedly, unpredictable future. The more he didn't want to believe, the more he knew that the only rational explanation was that the text he received had actually come from a higher being. How or why God would decide to communicate with him, and especially through his iPhone, he could not explain. But, he also couldn't deny it had happened. A potentially life-threatening event was avoided because he trusted the text message from I AM.

The rest of the week proceeded as normal and there were no further texts from I AM. David had no real weekend plans other than some light housework and gardening. However, in the back of his mind, the events earlier in the week were never far. He had no one to talk to because he feared that if he revealed any of the events, it could possibly put his sanity into question. Who would believe God had sent him text messages through his phone? It was hard enough even for him to believe it.

On Saturday morning, the next text from I AM arrived.

"They have good pancakes at Jimmy's Egg."

Great. What does that mean? Am I supposed to have breakfast at Jimmy's Egg and, by the way, to which Jimmy's Egg am I supposed to go? He knew of about three of these restaurants in his neighborhood.

Having no other plans, he decided to randomly pick one of the three restaurants to have breakfast. But, then he laughed at himself at the idea anything he was doing was even remotely related to the concept of random behavior. If this was truly God, then he had to trust whichever restaurant he chose was the one he was supposed to visit. This idea began to conflict with his concept of free will.

Was I choosing the restaurant or was God leading me to choose the restaurant and, therefore, I just have the illusion of free will? His mind swirled with implications and contradictions.

He drove to the Jimmy's Egg on MacArthur Boulevard since he had eaten there with friends in the past. As he drove up, he noticed the parking lot was full, as would be expected for a Saturday morning. Waiting to be seated, he stood looking around at the customers crowding the restaurant. There was the usual mix for a Saturday morning. Groups of old men wearing comfortable and well-worn clothes, no longer in need of impressing their group of longtime friends, and the younger athletic adults in their jogging suits, with the flushed cheeks left over from an early Saturday morning run. There were couples lost in the morning newspaper, and a few singles all reading a book or tablet to avoid the lonely fact that they were, in fact, alone. He made these observations while eating his pancakes.

His eye then fell on a young mother, probably mid-30's, who was looking at the paper with a pencil in hand, telegraphing her status as either a crossword puzzle enthusiast or someone looking for a job, circling the potentials. With her was a young girl, presumably her daughter, who was clearly bored with the situation and kept getting out of her seat to explore the gumball machine and other areas of interest.

Finishing his pancakes, he noted they did seem to be especially good that morning. He kept looking around for something, anything that would be a clue as to why he'd been asked to come to Jimmy's Egg. Maybe he'd picked the wrong Jimmy's Egg? He was preparing to leave when a new text came in. "Wait" was the only word on the phone's display. He was in the process of texting back a reply when a shadow fell across his table and he looked up into the eyes of a young girl, probably about eight-years-old. She was the one with the young woman engrossed in her paper. Although he had delivered thousands of babies, he knew nothing about children.

"Hello," he said with a forced smile.

She hesitated, and ran her finger around the outer edge of the table. "Hi, my name is Julia. Whatcha' doin'?"

Without hesitation and with more candor than he'd expected, he replied, "texting God".

The girl's eyes opened wide with disbelief and then became more focused. "Oh, you're just kidding me."

"No," he replied. "I'm not. God has been texting me for few days now." As soon as the words left his mouth, he realized how ludicrous this all seemed. If anyone else had said this to him, he would be ordering a psych evaluation. The girl looked at his face looking for a smile or any added telltale sign that he was kidding. They held each other's gaze for several seconds and when it was obvious he wasn't going to withdraw the statement, she asked him a question.

In a hushed voice reserved for churches or libraries, she asked him, "Ask God why my daddy left." The question caught him off guard and for several seconds he was dazed. He had no idea how to respond to the innocent but obviously heartfelt question of this young girl.

He stammered as he tried to find the correct words. "I'm not sure that it works that way."

The hopeful glow that had filled the young girl's eyes quickly faded as she walked back to her mother's table. Since he finished him breakfast, there was no reason to sit there any longer. He paid his check, gave his waitress a more than generous tip and left the restaurant.

* * *

THE REST OF THE WEEK WAS UNEVENTFUL WITH NO MORE text messages from I AM. It was Friday afternoon and he wasn't on call for the weekend, although he'd likely go in for one of his own patients' delivery if necessary. He was looking forward to a mindless weekend of college football, running a few errands, and attacking a stack of medical journals that had built up much too high. He was finishing the never-ending paperwork of his last patients and was starting to leave the office when his phone once signaled a new text message.

"Jimmy's Egg, Saturday. Try the blueberry muffins."

All week he'd thought about the previous Saturday morning. After he received the message to wait, the young girl had come up to him and had engaged him in conversation. Was that what he'd been waiting for? A random conversation with a random girl?

Saturday morning came and he thought about trying another Jimmy's Egg location but then thought better of it and returned to the same restaurant. Many of the same groups of customers were there with some small changes. There was a group of high school students in a booth huddling over textbooks and coffee, an older couple who looked married and bored with each other and, once again, there was the young woman and her daughter.

As he was waiting to be seated, he made eye contact with the young girl. She raised her hand and made a slight waving gesture to him. The only open table was one next to the woman and her daughter. He sat down, put in an order for coffee and a blueberry muffin, and was beginning to scanning the menu when he heard someone say, "Are you the jerk who told my daughter he was texting God?"

He looked up somewhat startled and saw the question had come from the mother of the young girl. She was probably in her mid-thirties, a little too thin for his liking, with short brown hair stopping at her shoulders. She had clear blue eyes which, at the moment, were angrily looking at him.

"Excuse me?" he replied.

"Are you the guy who told my daughter he was texting God?"

He looked around as if he were a butterfly trapped in the web of a spider. There was no easy escape. "Ah, er, yeah. That would be me," he confessed.

Her eyes were blazing with anger. "What in the hell were you thinking? Why would you say something like that to my daughter? She was upset for the rest of the day. It took several hours to convince her that, even if there was a God, he would not be texting someone at Jimmy's Egg. Why would you put such ideas into her head? Are you stupid or something?"

"Well, I'm definitely not stupid but sometimes I do dumb things. I guess, in retrospect, I shouldn't have said anything to her. I truly didn't mean to cause any distress to you or your daughter," he said with all sincerity.

The young girl was shifting nervously in her seat, obviously embarrassed about her mother's open assault on the unsuspecting diner. "Mom, it's okay. Let it go. Please?" she pleaded with her mother.

Her mother ignored her and, continuing, said, "I want you to tell her you were kidding about texting God. Tell her it was all a joke."

David put his head down and let out a deep sigh. There was a very long, uncomfortably long, pause. He then raised his eyes and met the mother's gaze and in the somber voice he reserved for telling patients bad news about cancer or nonviable pregnancies he replied, "I'm sorry, I can't do that".

"Why?" snapped the mother.

There was another long pause as he tried to find words that wouldn't make him sound like some crazy religious fanatic.

"So?" she prodded.

Another painfully long pause, and then he answered her saying, "I can't say it because it wouldn't be true."

"Christ, Jesus" the woman spat out. "You're one of those religious nuts aren't you? What are you? Jehovah Witness? Mormon? Church of the First Born?"

"No," he defended himself. "I don't even go to church, unless you count Christmas and sometimes Easter."

"So, you're trying to tell me that you text God?" she questioned with a condescending tone that cut like a scalpel.

"Well, I usually just respond to his text messages and now that you mention it, I find it strange that I've never even considered texting him or her first," replied David. "I wonder what that says about me."

"Maybe it says that you're holding onto a shred of sanity. Wait. Stop! I can't believe you have sucked me into this conversation with the assumption that God is actually texting you. Oh, you're good. You're clever. Whatever craziness you are into, just keep it away from my daughter. Okay? Right? End of conversation," she said definitively before walking back to her table.

He took his time eating his breakfast and watched as the woman and child left.

The week passed uneventfully until Thursday night around 9 p.m. His phone signaled another message and he saw it was from I AM. It simply read, "Go to Labor and Delivery now." He jumped into his car and headed towards the hospital. He called ahead to find out what was going on. The report he got was confusing. The nurse told him there were three patients in labor and they all looked good on the monitors. He briefly thought about turning around and heading back home, but he knew in his heart it would be the wrong decision.

As he walked onto the unit, the ward clerk said, "Good evening Dr. Miller. What are you doing here?"

He responded with nonchalance that he didn't really feel, "I was just in the neighborhood, so I thought I would drop by to see what was going on."

"Well we have two of Dr. Houck's patients in labor and one of Dr. O'Brien's. All of them are about 4-5 cm dilated and are on cruise control."

"Well then, I think I'll get a Coke for the road" he replied.

As he turned to head towards the kitchen, a nurse suddenly stuck her head out of room 341 and shouted, "We have heart tones down, and we are bleeding, call for help."

He rushed into the room and quickly assessed the situation. The amount of bleeding and the rock hard uterus indicated that the patient was abrupting and was having tectonic contractions. He gowned and gloved, examined the patient and found she was fully dilated and the head almost to the vaginal perineum. Houck, her physician, lived in suburbs and couldn't make it to the hospital for at least 25-30 minutes. He barked out orders to get the NICU staff into the room, to get a pair of Simpson forceps and to prepare for delivery. Luckily, this was the patient's third baby and the rigid contractions had pushed her to complete dilatation. With the skill that comes with years of practice, he correctly assessed the fontanelles for position, slipped on the right blade of the forceps and then the left blade and then with the appropriate downward traction, delivered the baby. Not missing a beat, he cleaned out the mouth and nose before handing the baby to the waiting NICU nursing staff. After a few tense moments, there was the reassuring cry of the healthy newborn.

Dr. Miller then turned and said to the patient, who along with her relatives, had been thrust into a state fear by the sudden sequence of events. In a calm voice, honed over the years, he said, "I'm sorry. I guess I should introduce myself. My name is Dr. Miller and I just happened to be here when your baby went into distress. Your doctor is on his way and should be here in a few minutes. I will deliver the placenta and if there's any repair needed, your physician will take care of that. Obviously, as you can hear, the baby sounds great and he'll be fine. Congratulations on your baby." There was a collective release of tension and even some smiles and exclamations of relief in the room as the patient and her family listened to the loud protestations coming from the newborn.

With that, he delivered the placenta and removed the gown and gloves which he had rapidly put on after entering the delivery room. He then walked out to the nurses' station where several nurses were huddled talking.

Tara, one of the older and more reliable nurses remarked, "Well Miller, it sure was lucky you just happened to be hanging around here tonight. What's up with that anyway? You never hang out if you don't have somebody in labor. Why were you here tonight?"

He tried to dodge the question and jokingly replied, "I'm trying to hone my psychic abilities."

Smiling as he left the unit, he met Dr. Houck who was rushing towards the patient's room and explained everything that had happened, and that the baby and mother were doing well. He was thanked profusely, before he walked off the unit, leaving the nurses to ponder what they had just seen.

Once home and sat down with a beer, he sent I AM a text. "Is this the way it is going to be? You sending me on urgent missions to save lives or to intervene in people's lives?"

No reply came and he was left questioning the future of the relationship with this all-knowing entity that, for whatever reason, had chosen him to fulfill its mission.

* * *

FRIDAY EVENING HE RECEIVED A MESSAGE THAT SIMPLY SAID "Jimmy's Egg, Saturday, 1:00".

Strange. Nothing about breakfast or biscuits and gravy or any of the usual suggestions.

The next day, he went to Jimmy's Egg at 1 p.m. The crowd was a little bit different from the usual morning grouping. The lunch hour was almost over and the customers were thinning out. There were several open tables and this time the waitress told him to sit anywhere. He picked a corner booth by the window that was somewhat isolated, allowing him to be alone with his thoughts. The waitress came by and took his order for a Diet Coke. He heard a flurry of activity and looked up to see the mother of Julia, the little girl who had spoken to him two weeks before, bursting through the door. She frantically looked around and when she caught sight of David, she came directly to his table and sat down wearing a shroud of frenzied panic.

"What the hell is going on? How are you doing this and why are you doing this?" she snapped at him.

"Excuse me. I'm not sure I know what you're talking about," he replied confused.

"Don't give me that bullshit. You know exactly what I'm talking about," she said in a voice that was angry but also a little scared. She watched him waiting for and explanation. None came.

"So you're saying that you didn't send me the text about the EpiPen?"

"No, I don't know what you're talking about," replied David trying to speak in a slow and steady tone to defuse the tension of the conversation.

"Well let me tell you what I'm talking about then," she spat out venomously. "This morning I got a text from someone who calls himself I AM stating I should take Julia's EpiPen with me today. She was born with severe peanut allergies. She's essentially grown out of them over the past couple of years with no allergic reactions. Julia was invited to a friend's house for a sleep over and they were just finishing breakfast when I arrived to pick her up. The mom, who had invited her, explained to me that they were trying some new flour she had found at a health food store. As we are talking,

I heard Julia gasping and I looked at her and saw that she was having an obvious anaphylactic reaction. We called 911 but because of the text message, I had brought her EpiPen with me. I used it and it probably saved her life."

"Wow," was the only thing that David could say.

"She was taken to the emergency room for observation. While she was being evaluated, I called a good friend of mine who works for my cell phone provider to ask him to look at my text message records to find out who had sent me the text about the EpiPen. He pulled my records and told me that there was no record of any text message being sent. I explained that I was looking at it on my cell phone as we were speaking and once again, he said that there is no record of any text message being passed through any known cell tower. He had no good explanation as to how I could get a text and there be no record of it. He hinted that it was impossible and kept asking me if I was sure that I had received the text," she went on to explain.

"I then decided to come to the restaurant on the off chance you might be here. Why are you here anyway? It's not your usual time" she questioned.

Without saying a word, he pulled up his text from I AM and showed it to her. Her eyes widened. "Jimmy's Egg 1:00".

"Good God, what is going on?" she almost whispered.

"Good God may be closer to the truth then you can imagine. Look, I'm a doctor. I see people all the time praying for miracles, and I very rarely see them happen. I guess I believe that there is a God in some form, but I'm definitely not someone you would consider to be religious. When I started getting these text messages, I didn't believe it either until it reached a point that there was no way of denying it. Something strange is going on here and at this point, all of the messages have been helpful and sometimes life-saving as in your case."

"But why us? Why now?" she asked.

"I have no idea", he replied. "I guess we could ask."

"I don't know. I'm almost afraid to. I mean, if I hadn't listened to the message and taken the EpiPen with me today, Julia might not have made it. I guess, I'm afraid to make whatever or whoever it is- God, Goddess, The Great Beyond or The Great Spirit angry by asking questions about what most people would consider to be a great blessing."

"Well, I will then."

As he reached for his phone, lying on the table, she reached across the table touching his hand lightly. "Are you sure about this?" she asked looking deep into his eyes.

"I think it will be all right." He paused and then asked, "By the way, what's your name?"

"Amanda, Amanda Barr", she replied.

"Well then, let's make it official." As he held out his hand he said, "Amanda, my name is David Miller. It's a pleasure to meet you," he said with a smile. They shook hands and he noted that the handshake lingered a little longer than expected. Almost embarrassed, she pulled back her hand.

To break the awkwardness of the moment, he picked up the cell phone and typed in the message "Why us? Why now?"

Almost as soon as the message was sent, a reply came back to his cell phone. "No one can reply that fast," remarked Amanda.

"I don't think we're dealing with just 'anyone'," he replied in all seriousness. He looked at the cell phone and slowly read the words aloud. "It says, 'you both were ready.'"

"It's kind of weird to think He knows that we're together right now. But, I guess if this is really happening, I shouldn't be too surprised. I wonder what he meant by "we were ready" she asked. Her previous tense shoulders now relaxed.

"I don't know. I'm having a period of my life where I've been asking the big questions. Why am I here? Is this all there is? Is there a God? Those kinds of big questions."

"I know exactly what you're talking about," she responded. "Since my husband left, I've been trying to get a good job to support Julia and myself. I have been asking the same types of questions. Why is this happening to me? Is there purpose to all of these things? Why do bad things happen to good people? A good friend of mine says that I am on a spiritual journey, whatever that means," she said shrugging her shoulders. "Well, I've got to get back to the hospital to pick up Julia. This has probably been the strangest day of my life."

As she got up to leave, David said, "I'm glad that Julia is doing ok. She seems like a great kid."

"She is," she agreed, a smile lighting up her face.

"Would you say 'hi' to Julia for me?"

"Sure, I'd be happy to." Then after a slight pause, Amanda asked, "Would you like to join me and Julia for breakfast next Saturday?"

Without hesitation, he replied, "Yes".

With a slight smile, she said, "Good. We'll see you about 8:00 then."

He watched her as she walked out of the restaurant and wondered if she would turn around and look back. She did.

He was almost startled when his phone once again signaled a new message. He looked down and saw a lone emoji.

"☺"

He smiled and put his phone away.

THE CLOUD

JIM SAUNDERS GLANCED UP AT THE SKY AS HE GOT INTO HIS '89 Honda Accord and pulled out of his driveway in Springfield, Illinois. It was another lazy summer day, and the sky was crystal blue with unlimited view, just the way he liked it. As Chief of Operations at the Springfield Airport, weather was always on his mind.

As he pulled up to the terminal, he again looked up at the sky and saw only a singular wisp of a cloud. In the summer, it was common to see small white cumulus clouds appear in early morning, only to later burn off during the heat of the day. Sometimes they grew and turned into dark cumulonimbus forms bringing the thunderstorms the Midwest states were noted for. This looked like one of the days when the clouds would disappear under the sun's rays. It was going to be another perfect summer day, he thought, as he opened the door to the terminal.

* * * * *

HARVEY WALLER INSPECTED THE FLIGHT PLAN HANDED TO him by his co-pilot, Don Booker. Harvey was a 56-year-old pilot who'd been flying for over thirty-five years. He'd learned to fly at the end of Korean War and had seen some action in Vietnam before becoming a commercial pilot. He used to fly for the larger airlines, but, as he got older, he found his nature suited the smaller commuter lines and was quite content to go at a slower pace until the time came when he could retire. Don was the opposite. He was young and trying to get enough hours logged so he could get his rating for the larger planes. Harvey was on the down slope and Don was on the way up, and on a summer's day in early June, their paths crossed.

* * * * *

JIM WALKED THROUGH THE TERMINAL AS HE USUALLY DID, to get a feel for how things were going. He could sense tension when planes were delayed and employees' nerves frayed, or the calm excitement that occurred when passengers were getting ready to fly. Little kids liked to watch the planes land and take off, and he could see the smudges of their fingers and noses on the glass windows facing the runway. Springfield didn't get any of the large planes unless they were diverted and had to land due to weather or a fuel shortage. Today there was the typical steady stream of commuter flights as they stopped to pick up passengers before heading to the larger St. Louis, Dallas, or Denver hubs.

Jim left the terminal and made the short walk outside to the control tower where his office was located. He glanced up at the sky and noticed the wispy cloud had not dissipated but had, in fact, become thicker to the point he could just barely see the blue sky through it. It had also developed an almost circular shape about it. *Strange*, he thought. He walked over to the panel where the weather instruments displayed their continuous flow of information. Wind out of the west/northwest, humidity low, and barometer steady. Nothing that should worry him. The cloud must have been caught in a windless area that occurred between air patterns. Still, it should have burnt off by now. A small wrinkle of worry formed across his forehead.

* * * * *

HARVEY SETTLED BACK TO RELAX. THE TAKE-OFF HAD GONE smoothly, so he was letting Don fly the plane and, like a young puppy, he enthusiastically took over the controls. It was a short hop from Joplin to Springfield, and then on to St. Louis. The plane was about half-full, and with the passengers they would pick up in Springfield, they would almost have a full load, which was what the home company liked. If things went well, he would be home in time for dinner with his wife and three children.

* * * * *

JIM WALKED UP THE STAIRS LEADING TO THE CONTROL tower. When he had time, he liked to come to the tower to hang out with the controllers. They were a bright bunch of men and women, and he liked the feeling of being able to see the entire airport.

"How are things going?" he asked, walking to the large window overlooking the runway.

"The morning rush is over and we're just waiting for the last commuter flight coming in from Joplin," answered Stan Korvorski, the old Control Chief who had worked in this tower for more than twenty years. Stan had started as a maintenance worker in his teens, then as a controller, and finally as Control Chief whose job it was to oversee the other controllers. He saw his job as a juggler, moving people and planes while making everything look smooth and effortless. He walked over to where Jim was looking out the window.

"What are you looking at so intently?" he asked.

"Oh, nothing. Just a weird little cloud that hasn't moved since I saw it this morning when I got into my car," Jim replied.

"That's strange," Stan said glancing out at the white wisp. Clouds didn't usually stay in one position for very long due to the many changing air currents in the atmosphere. He looked more closely at the cloud capturing Jim's attention. It was about 4,000 feet high and about 400 feet in diameter. *That* is *odd,* Stan thought. The cloud had distinct edges and not the feathery nature common in this type of formation.

"Strange color, too," he added, almost as an afterthought.

That's right, Jim thought. The cloud had developed almost a luminous hue as if it were lit from the inside.

"I don't like it," Jim said, the wrinkles in his forehead deepening.

"Well, it's just a cloud, and as long as it doesn't get any bigger and turn into a thunder storm, it shouldn't cause us any problems."

"I don't know," Jim said, letting his words trail off.

＊ ＊ ＊ ＊ ＊

"ABOUT TIME WE GET CLEARANCE FOR LANDING," HARVEY SAID.

"Right." Don flicked a few switches. "This is Delta 6133 out of Joplin, requesting final clearance for landing."

"Roger, Delta 6133. This is Springfield Tower. You'll be coming in on runway number two. I repeat number two. Change to heading 212 and prepare for your final descent."

"Roger, we copy that. We are now reading 212 and have runway two in sight. We should be on the ground in a few minutes," Don answered before he ceased transmission. "Do you want to take back the controls," he asked Harvey as a courtesy.

"No, just don't bounce us," Harvey joked.

＊ ＊ ＊ ＊ ＊

JIM HEARD THE TOWER CONVERSATION AS HE HAD HUN-dreds of times in the past, but today something was different. Something wasn't right. He had a feeling he'd come to trust over the years. The feeling you get when you come home and sense something in your house is out of place without being able to put your finger on what it is. Something wasn't right. He was sure of it. But what it was, he did not know.

And then the cloud began to move.

"Well, your cloud is finally drifting away," Stan joked, his eyes glancing over to the weather instrument panel. "That's weird," he said, almost to himself.

"What is it?" asked Jim.

"The wind is out of the northwest but the cloud is drifting into the wind. That shouldn't happen. *Jesus*, would you look at that," he said, shifting his attention from the dials to the cloud.

The cloud had changed to a brighter white and had a glow as if you were looking at the sun thru it, though this was not the case. The edges had sharpened up and it was drifting on a course intersecting with Flight 6133.

* * * * *

"HARVEY."

"I know. I see it." He instinctively put his hand back on the plane's controls without taking control. They were both looking at a strange cloud drifting into their flight path. It was too late to avoid it, except with an emergency maneuver not called for in this situation. Not to avoid a cloud. Still, in all of his years of flying, he had never seen a cloud with such sharp and distinct lines. And the light. It looked like it was reflecting the sun's light back at them, but the angle of the sun wasn't right for that to occur. Not knowing why, he took over control of the plane as they began to enter the cloud.

On the ground, Jim and Stan watched as Delta Flight 6133, entered into the cloud. It would come out on the other side in just a few seconds, Jim thought, but the hairs on the back of his neck were standing up.

* * * * *

AS DELTA FLIGHT 6133 ENTERED THE CLOUD, A STRANGE HUSH came over the plane. Harvey noticed the plane's engines had a faraway, muffled sound. The controls felt very smooth in his hands, as if they were in a very calm patch of air. He couldn't see beyond the windshield. Even the nose of the plane wasn't visible.

"What the..." he exclaimed. The compass started spinning wildly. The altimeter was bouncing all over the scale, and from the trim control, he couldn't tell if they were flying right side up or upside down. Then he heard the hum as he reached for the radio.

* * * * *

IN THE TOWER, EVERYONE HEARD THE SPEAKERS. "CONTROL, this is Del… *crackle* we are… *pop*... prob… struments… readings… confused." And then nothing.

"Where are they? They should have come out by now. It's not that big," Jim said with a touch of panic in his voice.

"They're off the screen," Stan said looking at the tower's main radar screen. "What?"

"They were there and now they're just gone."

"That's impossible they can't 'just be gone'. They can't."

But they were. Commuter Flight 6133 out of Joplin had disappeared. No wreckage. No plane. No people. Nothing to ever show the flight with its five crew members and 47 passengers ever existed.

THE HISTORY OF CATCH
AND RELEASE

THE HISTORY OF THE CATCH AND RELEASE PROGRAM BEGAN
with the discovery of planet Episthaleon-3461, also known by the native
term Earth, by the legendary xeno-explorer Shalabith Notir.

When the first xenobiologists began to characterize the life forms
of E-3461, it was noted that the amount of genetic diversity placed it in
the top one percent of known planets. There was a footnote mention of a
biped life form showing rudimentary tool development, as well as the ability to make crude line drawings of native animals on the walls of the caves
they inhabited.

The next mention was after 30,000 rotations or years of E-3461
around its central sun, when a hyperbaric transport made an emergency
stop to refill the ship's water supply for its hydrogen fusion engines. The
captain made mention of a budding society which fulfilled the definition
of a civilization since it demonstrated writing, maintained a ceremonial
center structure, and was organized into a city. This notation was filed

away in the archives until it was rediscovered approximately 1,025 E-3461 years later by a student who was working on his thesis about high diversity planets. The discovery of a civilization having developed in such a short course of time intrigued the scientific community, which prompted the first research expedition to study the advanced lifeforms of E-3461.

This resulted in the first comprehensive study of E-3461. Many different research studies on the dominant species, known as humans, were performed. In these early years, regulations were few and the biologists were free to harvest as many specimens as they desired for anatomical and physiological studies. One of the most controversial studies involved researchers identifying themselves to the local inhabitants as demi-gods. In this experiment, multiple early civilizations were given instructions on how to build a four-sided polyhedron. The researchers then recorded how each separate culture interpreted the "will of the gods" and how each polyhedron was built. This was the largest field experiment in the history of xenobiology and was conducted over several thousands of E-years.

The rapid cultural changes of E-3461 turned the planet into a popular vacation destination, as well as a field research lab. Depending on the season, one could expect to see different factions warring, which made for an exciting family get away. During this time, it was common for travel merchants to wager on the outcome of conflicts and there was a strong suspicion they sometimes intervened to ensure exotic entertainment for their clients. This activity was later brought under control by Anti-Interference Regulations which forbade the directing or influencing of normal cultural development.

No discussion of the Catch and Release Program would be complete without the mention of the illegal trade of members in the dominant species, known as humans. Wealthy patrons were known to collect the dominant lifeforms, with the goal of having a breeding pair from each continent. These animals did not adapt well to captivity. They were fiercely independent. Despite having cages with all the best accommodations, this species would constantly strive to escape, sometimes causing harm to their owners. Their short life spans averaged 60 E-years which required that the illegal collections had to be continually updated with new stock. Human infants did not thrive in captivity and were sometimes killed by their own brood pair. The trafficking in these exotic animals, although outlawed, still continues today.

Catch and Release Regulations-version 17.217

To protect the diverse natural resources of E-3461, we request the cooperation and responsible actions of all citizens to allow for a regulated trapping of desired species.

Extreme caution should be practiced when attempting to trap the human prey. In the past, they were relatively harmless as long as one remained watchful for flying projectiles such as rocks and wooden shafts tipped with sharpened animal bones. They have now reached the technological point where they can cause significant damage with a range of moderately sophisticated weapons. Several citizen trappers have been injured or killed when they let down their guard as well as their personal protective fields. This program shall not be responsible for any injury, maiming, loss of limb or life of any citizen choosing to attempt the trapping of this species.

The Catch and Release Program continues to grow and strengthen with new trappers taking up this time-honored tradition, but only when doing so with the help and guidance of knowledgeable, seasoned trappers. With this strong mentoring system, new trappers learn about the basic biology of humans and the role of humans in the historical development of E-3461. New trappers should be educated in responsible management, trapper ethics, and trapper responsibilities.

No age restrictions apply to the Catch and Release Program as it applies to the capture of humans. Due to the potential damage caused by the misuse the standard immobilization beam, the young trapper must be of legal age and have completed approved mentoring. For more information, visit *dnr.wi.C&R*; keywords: 'mentored catch and release'. All trappers must obtain a trapping license regardless of age. A trapper must have reached the minimum age of 10 years, successfully completed a Catch and Release Program and have appropriate adult supervision. These courses are offered through the Division of Exotic Wildlife.

All first-time trappers must complete the Galactic Catch and Release course prior to purchasing a license. A certificate of successful completion of the Galactic Catch and Release education course may be used by a resident in place of a trapping license for the year in which the certificate is issued.

Trapping is now allowed on most continents with exceptions, which will be discussed in paragraph 8.

It is illegal to set, place, or operate any holographic projection device with the purpose of attracting or coercing said specimens into a legally sanctioned containment field. Baiting of humans by any means is prohibited.

Standard immobilization beams shall be used for all captures as they have demonstrated a low risk of damage to the human, as long as they are well-maintained and used at the appropriately sanctioned power settings. Use of older techniques such as paralytic gases, stun rods, or freeze rays is strictly prohibited. Use of these illegal capture techniques should be reported immediately. (reference paragraph 11)

If incidental catch of a protected species occurs (i.e. rare native inhabitants of the land mass known by humans as the Amazon rainforest), please contact your local Conservation Warden as soon as possible for instructions on how to release an endangered species. A protected species is any for which the season is closed, there is no open season, or no authorization to possess has been granted.

Trapping on or over heavily populated lands and water is not allowed under the regulations of the program. Open contact with humans on a large scale is forbidden as it has been shown to cause significant distress for the species. (reference Orson Wells, 1938) Posted rules may require written authorization to trap in some areas or may specify other restrictions.

It is lawful to set traps in open water as this method has been shown to be very productive in obtaining small groups of humans without having to risk being discovered by the species at large. Catch limit for open water is not to exceed six.

It is lawful to set traps in the lower atmosphere as long as the capture occurs over water or a sparsely populated land mass and the acquired flying vehicle carries no more than six specimens as seizing larger vehicles increases the risk of herd panic. (reference paragraph 6)

It is mandated that the trapper must perform the standard Memsweep procedure on all specimens before releasing them back into their environment. Failure to do so increases the risk of panicking the population thus making it more difficult for future trappers. Versions of Memsweep older than Memsweep 118.23.974 should not be used as the older versions have been shown to allow capture memory recall under conditions of extreme relaxation, neural recall techniques and certain species-specific drugs.

Tagging specimens with neural implants for research and migration studies is allowed.

Support Ethical Responsible Trapping •
Report Violations

Use Temporal link: WDNR (1-800000-847-9367; toll free), or

#367 from your trans-galactic com. **Note:** This is **NOT** an information number.

TransWarpTEXT: Text a tip to TIP-411 (847-411)

Standard text rates apply.

Have a great time out there! Learn new skills, respect others' needs, and take a friend or family member with you. Through your responsible actions, non-trappers will have a greater appreciation of what makes an ethical trapper one of the finest xeno-naturalists in our star quadrant. Prior to, during, and after the catch and release season, act as if the future of trapping depends on your actions – because it does!

Have a safe, productive and memorable experience.

THE DARK

FROM THE MOMENT JOHN CARPENTER OPENED HIS EYES, HE knew something was wrong. His bedroom was lit with the early morning sunlight, indicating he'd overslept. He never used an alarm clock. Instead, he relied on the usual morning sounds of the roosters, cows, and barking dogs that surrounded him on his Oklahoma ranch. This morning, there were no sounds. The sun coming in through the faded curtains of his sparsely furnished bedroom meant it must be around eight in the morning. As he moved to get dressed, he couldn't help feeling unsettled by the lack of animal sounds with which he was so familiar.

His ranch consisted of 360 acres, east of Woodward, Oklahoma, much of which he now leased out to other farmers and ranchers who wanted to run their own livestock. His three children had all left the ranch, as this was not a lifestyle they wanted. He still ran his own small herd of beef cattle, but after the death of his wife and the departure of his children, his heart was no longer into the work of ranching. John loved the land and the independence that came from living on his own, but with no one to share the land with or to pass it on to, his passion had burnt out long ago.

He lived a lifestyle greatly unchanged in the last hundred years. He had a small garden he tended and enough livestock to take care of his needs. Most of his time was spent in maintenance of the farm and, as with most aging farms, there was always work to do. His closest son had moved to Oklahoma City, and while the drive between their places was a short two hours, they only got together about twice a year, usually on holidays. The other two children had left Oklahoma for the brighter lights of the west coast. His wife had died three years earlier of cancer and, without her as his foundation, he was alone and lost as a children's balloon, escaped from a party and last seen floating into the sky.

That morning, he dressed in common, comfortable clothes, consisting of his favorite work boots, a fairly clean pair of blue jeans, and a fresh shirt. On his face was a gray scruffy beard, which he briefly considered shaving but then decided not to. What was the point? He walked downstairs and noted the banister was getting loose. One more item he'd have to put on his list of things to do. He made himself his usual breakfast of bacon, eggs, and hot coffee. It was the early spring and was still chilly so he put on his light jean jacket and walked out his front door to face the day.

Standing on the porch holding his coffee, he once again noticed the silence of the usually noisy farmyard. He walked to the chicken coop and saw all the chickens sitting on their nests in a position that usually meant a storm was coming. Lifting his head at the sky and in the east, towards the town of Woodward, he could see a low bank of clouds coming in his direction. The clouds were dark and extended across the horizon, but he could still see blue sky above them. These were typical of the quickly forming thunderclouds that developed over the prairies of Oklahoma. While most storm clouds were a dark gray, he noted that this wall of clouds was black, a color he had never recalled seeing before. He figured it must be one hell of a storm coming his direction.

He walked to the barn, and, like the chickens, he found the horses lying in their stalls, which was strange. His horses would usually paw the dirt, neigh incessantly, buck, and roll on the ground with approaching bad weather. John had never seen them go and lie down in their stalls. He remembered once he'd seen a few wild Mustangs trapped out on the prairie as a tornado approached. They laid down on the stomachs with their heads facing away from the oncoming tornado. This was the position he found his own horses in now.

He left the barn and looked to the east, toward Woodward to see the dark wall of clouds was closer than before. Unlike the formation of clouds suggesting the arrival of a tornado, these clouds didn't have a circular rotation pattern. He reached in his pocket and pulled out his cell phone. It was one of the few modern conveniences he allowed himself. Several times he had found the phone to be an important part of ranching, as it allowed him to call the vet if a cow was down out on the range or the feed store if he needed extra supplies for the winter.

He decided to call Bill Hastings, the owner of the largest feed store in Woodward. John had known Bill all his life as they'd gone to the same schools for twelve years. Bill was probably the closest person John considered as a friend. The phone connected with Bill, but a recording stating the number he'd called was not working or was no longer in service was the answer. He thought he must have misdialed and called the feed store once again. The message was the same. His next call was to Arnold Shoemaker, the large animal veterinarian servicing his county. When he heard the same out of service phone message, a strange sense of fear passed over him. He stood looking towards the east at the large dark cloud covering the town of Woodward.

As a reserve Deputy Sheriff for the city of Woodward, John had a police band radio in his pickup truck. He went to his truck and powered up the radio, but when he keyed the microphone, all he got was static. He tried the emergency bands, weather bands, and CB bands, all with the same result, all with the same static. It was as if the town of Woodward no longer existed. An involuntary shudder went down his spine.

To the east, the dark black wall had come significantly closer. It didn't have the normal variations in tone like a dark wall cloud as a thunderstorm approached. It was a sheet of black extending almost from horizon to horizon. A small strip of clear blue sky could still be seen over the blackness.

He decided he would drive towards Woodward to see what was wrong. He wondered if there had been some type of natural gas explosion or a train derailment with chemical fires causing the ominous billowing black smoke.

He turned on the ignition of his pickup truck and waited for his dog to join him. Buck was a mongrel mix of German Shepherd and some other unknown breed who had wandered onto the homestead two years before. Both human and dog were hesitant of each other in the beginning, but had one thing in common, loneliness. Over time, a bond of friendship had developed and Buck was now a common sight riding in the pickup truck with John. The sound of the engine turning over usually brought Buck running to the truck. Not this time. John got out of the truck, leaving the engine running, and called for Buck. There was no sight of the dog, but John heard a whimper from underneath the front porch of the house. He got down on his hands and knees but couldn't see into the darkness, so he made a quick trip back to his pickup truck to retrieve the flashlight he always kept with him. He used one of the newer flashlights that produced 3,000 lumens from a high-intensity discharge Xenon lamp which allowed him to see cattle up to a half mile away. It had been very useful on many a stormy night when he was out looking for lost livestock.

On his hands and knees, John shone the bright light underneath the porch. He saw Buck lying there. The dog didn't appear to be injured, and when John called to the dog, Buck crawled out from underneath the porch, and laid at his feet shivering with his tail tucked between his legs as if in stark fear. John couldn't get his dog to jump into the pickup truck with him and he worried Buck might be ill. This was something he would check out after he returned from Woodward. It was just another strange event he added to the many that had happened since he'd awoken. The horses, poultry, and now the dog were acting in ways he'd never seen in over fifty years of living on the farm. Somehow, he knew it had something to do with the wall of blackness headed in his direction.

Back in his pickup truck, for a moment John had a fearful thought he should be driving away from the cloud, not toward it. He pushed the thought from his mind and headed toward town. As he got closer, the black wall kept getting taller and taller until he could no longer see any blue sky above it. When he topped the hill, what he saw caused him to bring the truck to a screeching stop. Across a small valley, he could clearly see the black wall, slowly moving his direction But he couldn't see anything through it. If this was a cloud, he should have been able to see the outline of trees or the road where it entered into the wall of blackness. But there was nothing. It was as if the dark wall was devouring everything it encountered, as if it were a living entity. For the first time, John felt the same fear he'd seen in his livestock. He was not a religious man, but he had the sense he was looking at pure evil. The type of evil which came from hell itself.

Part of him wanted to run. But something about the entity was calling him to get closer to the dark cloud. He couldn't resist, although it terrified him. He slowly released the brake and the truck moved forward toward the dark.

He stopped his truck, about fifty feet from the wall of darkness, which was creeping toward him. He had his flashlight with him and he slowly walked towards the dark trying to peer inside of it with his Xenon flashlight. The beam of light could clearly be seen but it didn't reflect off, nor did it penetrate, the dark. It was as if the darkness was consuming the light. He slowly approached the dark with his flashlight held out far in front of him. The closer John got to the dark, the more he knew he was sensing evil and the more he was drawn to it. It may have been his imagination, but he thought the movement of the dark slowed as he approached it, as if it were waiting for him. He tentatively held his flashlight to the dark, which was now only inches away from the lens. As the edge of the flashlight came into contact with the dark, the entire length of the flashlight became encrusted in frost, as if it had come into contact with a sub-zero environment. The edge of the flashlight was now in the dark but he could not see the light beam nor the edge of the flashlight. He tried to pull the flashlight free of the dark but it felt as if something was holding it and pulling from the other side.

He let go the flashlight and quickly backed away. As he did, the dark began to move forward once again, slowly. The flashlight was being held by some invisible force and within a few seconds, it was swallowed by the dark. He turned and ran as fast as he could back to his still running pickup truck. Throwing the truck in reverse, John drove backwards until he could find a turnaround. With his truck now heading away from the dark, he drove as fast as he could to try to put as much distance between him and the dark as possible. As he was speeding away he could feel the dark calling to him, pulling him back. In the depth of his soul, he knew running was futile. The evil he felt from his brief contact with the dark was so palpable he knew he was witnessing the beginning of the end.

THE DEVIL'S DELIVERY

"THE STRANGEST DELIVERY I EVER HAD WAS IN THE EARLY 80's, a couple living on some type of hippie commune farm outside of Columbia, Missouri," said Dr. Brown. He was sitting in the physician's lounge with several other physicians playing their favorite game of, "let's see you top that."

The other contestants consisted of two younger physicians, Dr. Bradford and Dr. Hyde. The three obstetricians were sitting around a table drinking bad lounge coffee and nibbling on stale muffins.

"Well," continued Dr. Brown, "they heard that skin-to-skin contact was good for the baby so they assumed it would be good for the mother. When the nurse and I walked in, we found the wife in labor and naked, sandwiched between her husband and the female doula who were also naked."

"You're kidding," exclaimed Dr. Bradford.

"No. It didn't bother me, but we had a difficult time finding nurses who could handle that much skin."

"Great story," said Dr. Hyde. "If you guys ever get the chance, you need to ask Dr. Kay about the time he snuck a gorilla in to the OR on a Sunday to perform infertility surgery for the zoo. Those were the good ol' days when medicine was more like the Wild West."

There was a pause as they sipped their coffee. From behind, they heard a gruff voice say, "I delivered the Devil's child." Startled, they turned to see Dr. Graystone, sitting alone at a table sipping his tea.

"Yeah," responded Dr. Hood, "we've all had patients who are mean and nasty, just evil."

"You got that right," chimed Dr. Bradford.

Dr. Graystone kept stirring his tea, not looking up. He was the last of the old school obstetricians. No one knew how old he was, but they suspected he was in his seventies, and he was one of the last doctors to still be in solo practice. His wife had died years before and his children were grown and had moved away. His life, his last love, was being an obstetrician. His skill with forceps was legendary, verging on magical. He scoffed at the younger physicians who would refer their gestational diabetics to endocrinologist or sent every patient with palpitations for cardiac workup. But when there was an emergency and the patient was bleeding out, he was the one they always called first. Many a scared physician had looked up with a sense of relief as they saw Dr. Graystone walking in to the OR with his hands held high, still dripping from the washing. He would always begin, "Well, what do we have today," with a calm that only came from years of practice and over 9,000 deliveries. The other doctors' and nurses' nickname for him was The Lone Ranger because he was the masked man who always came to the rescue.

In the lounge, the doctors waited for a smile or wink from Dr. Graystone, but it never came. They remained in a respectful silence still not knowing if they were about to hear a story or joke.

"I did my internship in Grand Forks, North Dakota, 90 miles from the Canadian border. A miserable place," he said reverently stirring his tea.

He still hadn't looked up. "It was a small program, and we only had two residents at each level. Part of our duties was to cover the SAC Air Force Base outside of town.

"SAC?" asked Dr. Hyde.

"Strategic air command," interjected Dr. Brown.

"Yes," said Dr. Graystone. There was a long, almost painful pause as if he were dusting off an old memory to recount. "In those days, interns took call in house by themselves."

"You're kidding," exclaimed Dr. Bradford. "No attendings? No senior residents?"

"No, if you needed help you could call someone, but they were fifteen minutes away and in case of a blizzard, you were on your own"

"Crap," murmured Dr. Hyde, "that's hard-core."

"That night, there was a thunderstorm that can only happen on the plains. It came up fast and mean with thunder that sounded like an artillery barrage in Vietnam. The power was out and we were on backup generators. The emergency lighting painted everything with an orange, eerie glow. A patient was brought in by the MP's. She was found in a stalled car outside of the main gate, and even though this was a secured base, they brought her to the hospital since she was obviously in active labor."

The physicians lounge had become very quiet, and several other physicians had stopped to listen to the story.

Dr. Graystone continued. "They brought her straight to the delivery room. We didn't use birthing rooms in those days, everyone delivered on an OR table. I checked the patient and she was completely dilated and a +2 station. The nurse and I quickly put her in stirrups. She had dark, dirty, stringy hair and eyes that seem to have a glow; you know the kinda red glow you see if you shine light in the eyes of a wild animal. Her body was covered in tattoos, but not the kind that we all see. They were symbols that looked like hieroglyphics and they covered most of her skin. She was chanting some phrase over and over, and at first, I thought that she must be post ictal from an eclamptic seizure."

A nurse entered the lounge and said, "Dr. Brown, they're ready for you in room five."

He brushed her off with a curt, "Tell them I'll be there in a few minutes."

Dr. Graystone slowly scanned the room making eye contact with all of the physicians, looking at them above his heavy turtle shell glasses that hadn't been in style since the 70's. "She was writhing on the bed, and I was afraid she was going to throw herself off.

A few of the doctors had now moved to sit down at the old man's table. "Then what?" asked Dr. Brown.

"Yes, what?" Dr. Graystone said cryptically, as he continued to sip his tea.

"When she crowned, her membranes ruptured. At first I thought it was thick meconium, but it was a black foul-smelling fluid with the stench of an E. coli abscess. I thought she must have had an infected stillbirth but the monitor was still picking up a heartbeat. The lights in the room started flickering off and on. I was sure we were going to lose power.

"She started screaming in what sounded like she was speaking in tongues, the orations you might hear in a Pentecostal revival. The head delivered and its hair was dark but coarse, the kind an animal would have. I stuck my fingers into the mouth and was attempting to remove the black scum when the baby bit me."

There was a small chuckle from several other physicians.

With no smile or smirk, he continued. "Blood started pouring out of my finger. The baby had a razor sharp beak instead of gums. I screamed and fell back against the wall. The nurse tried to help but the patient back-handed her and she fell against the wall, hitting her head, knocking herself unconscious. The scrub tech ran out of the room screaming."

"Oh, come on," said Dr. Hood in disbelief.

Dr. Graystone just stared at him through the thick glasses with an unwavering look and kept speaking. "The patient sat up on the table, reached down and grabbed her baby's head and with one final scream, she pulled the child out. I was over in the corner, clutching my mangled finger, watching all of this happen. She bit down on the umbilical cord, crimping it off before chewing through it."

The doctor's lounge was silent as everyone listened to the story with an intensity seldom found among physicians.

"She then held the baby up with both hands and spoke in English this time. "Satan, here is your child. I offer him to you."

There was a pause as he sipped his tea and then continued.

"There was a dull orange glow on the floor at the foot of the OR table, and the floor turned into a pool of swirling light. Then a creature or being came up from the pool of light. I can only assume it was the Devil."

"Bullshit," said Dr. Bradford, but the icy glare from Dr. Graystone cut his words out of the air like a scalpel.

"This being, this *thing* had a very indistinct form, as if it were made up of smoke and shadow which were continually changing its shape. But it was large. It took the baby and cradled it in one arm. Then it touched the patient on the forehead and she fell back on the table. It turned to me and I thought I was going to die. Then suddenly, the swirling light went out and it was gone, taking the baby with it.

"When the scrub tech arrived with help, the patient was unconscious on the table. All of the tattoos and symbols were gone from her skin. The patient had no memory of who she was or how she had gotten there. And, there were no signs she had ever been pregnant."

"What about the placenta?" quipped Dr. Hood. "That was proof that she had a baby."

"There was no placenta. As I said, there was no sign that she was ever pregnant. There was a big investigation since this was a high security missile base. The pathology lab couldn't identify the black goo from the floor. They tried to write it off as some type of hallucination, but they couldn't explain the fetal monitor strip with the time and date stamps showing that some infant had been on the monitor."

The three younger doctors looked at each other, not knowing what to say. The tension was broken as a nurse stuck her head in the door. "Dr. Graystone, they're ready for you in room 10."

"Thank you," he said.

He stood up to leave and pushed his thick glasses up higher on the bridge of his nose with his middle finger, as his index finger was missing down to the second knuckle.

THE IT GUY

WHEN HE OPENED HIS EYES FOR THE FIRST, HE WAS SEVERELY disoriented. All he could see was a low metal ceiling crisscrossed with ducts and piping of varying sizes. At first he thought he was paralyzed, until he discovered he could move his fingers and toes. The energy for lifting up an arm or leg was non-existing. After much effort, he turned his head to the right and saw he was in a medical exam room filled with equipment. He recognized a cryopod, EKG machine and defibrillator. A bag of IV fluid running through a humming pump was draining into his right forearm.

He could see that he was not alone. There was another person sitting at a desk with their back to him wearing what looked to be some type of medical uniform. He tried to speak but only a gurgling noise came out. The man, who looked to be in his late forties, poured a clear liquid from a silver flask into a metal cup with a straw and brought it to him.

"Hold on cupcake. Don't try to talk until you get some fluid into you," the man said in a raspy voice. A slight odor of antiseptic was detected. "You've been asleep a long time. Don't try to move. Your muscles are too weak, but you're not paralyzed and your strength will come back in a few days. I know you have a thousand questions, but right now you need to rest. We'll talk later.

He closed his eyes and tried to focus.

I am…? I am…? He thought.

Devon McAdams was the answer which came to him slowly like a bubble that broke from the ocean floor and worked itself to the surface with a burst of memory. This revelation drained his meager energy. He drifted back to sleep, a sleep filled with flashes of dream fragments and hollow words.

When he opened his eyes again, he had no idea how long he'd been asleep but he found his mind was clearer and he was able to begin focusing his thoughts. He began to retrace the actions that brought him to this bed. Memories began to coalesce. He remembered driving home from work. Work? His work had something to do with computers. No, not just computers. The hacking of computers. That was what he was. He was a computer hacker.

A small sense of achievement came over him as if he had found the corner pieces of a jigsaw puzzle.

He had been driving home from work and…and… then there was a light.

A light? His mind toyed with the cheesy science fiction idea that he was involved in some type of alien abduction. But the man he'd talked to seemed obviously human, so he quickly kicked that idea to the curb. Also, the more he thought about the light, the more he remembered there were people associated with the light. Some type of police official?

He returned to a fitful sleep.

When he next awoke, the man he'd met before was present and once again brought him fluids to drink. After several swallows of a fluid he was sure was laced with some type of medicine or vitamin combination, he felt strong enough to voice a question.

"Where am I?" he slurred. "Who are you?"

"You can call me Doc. Everyone does. I'm going to raise the head of the bed. You let me know if it makes you feel lightheaded or nauseated."

The words Zheleznaya Ptitsa were embroidered on Docs jacket. *Zheleznaya Ptitsa is Russian for iron bird*, he thought. How did he know that?

The sound of an old electric motor started and the bed creaked as it raised him into a sitting position.

"Zheleznaya Ptitsa," he croaked in a harsh voice.

"Yeah. I was ferried over from the Zhel to help begin the activation protocol." He paused, then continued. "According to my records," Doc said looking at a computer screen, "you are Devon McAdams. Computer procurer for the Turn Corporation. Does that sound about right?"

Computer procurer. Turn Corporation. At first these words seemed to him muddy fragments, but their context became clearer as memories began to return and more pieces of the puzzle formed.

The Turn Corporation was the largest deep space mining conglomeration in the neo-Eastern Bloc State, which was a coalition of the old states of Uzbekistan, Kazakhstan, and much of old eastern Russia. They had pioneered the field of deep space mining and had almost a complete monopoly on the rare metals financial sector, as much of the world's economy was dependent upon the ore they brought back from their explorations.

The Turn Corporation didn't have much of a reputation when it came to corporate ethics. This allowed it to flourish in the Eastern Bloc where officials turned a blind eye if the money was good.

So, he remembered what the Turn Corporation was; now he just had to remember what a 'computer procurer' was.

"Is it coming back to you?" asked Doc.

"Some. Can I have some more to drink?"

"Sure," replied Doc as he brought him the cup again. "It is a mixture of electrolytes, amino acids and vitamins all designed to kick start your body."

"Thanks," he said after a few swallows. "I was a computer procurer?"

"Or a computer impressment officer. Whichever you prefer. You were one of the best, from what I've heard."

Impressment was the old English term for taking men into a military or naval service by compulsion, with or without notice.

Like a dam bursting, all of the pieces of the puzzle started coming together. The Turn Corporation made its fortune sending out deep space mining expeditions that lasted almost 50 years. The crew and miners would be placed in cryo-stasis for the first 20 years of the enterprise, at which point they would be revived or activated. They would then conduct their mining operations until the cargo bays were full, which usually took five to seven years. At that time, they would return to cryo-stasis for the 20 year return journey.

It took a special type of crew for these half century long journeys. Generally, they had to be men with no connections, because most everyone they knew before leaving the solar system would likely be dead by the time they returned home. The money was that of fables, and a single trip would allow a person to retire in the excess of luxury. Some men would also place their families in cryo-stasis, but for the most part, the crews were single men.

The time sacrifice of an expedition made it difficult to find enough miners who would voluntarily sign on. So the Turn Corporation experimented with the idea of offering these employment slots to prisoners with life sentences. It was decided that the years in cryo-stasis would meet the qualifications for life imprisonment. As with many ideas that originate from a corporate boardroom, this one ended in disaster when the deep space ship, Stanovoy, returned on autopilot with the discovery that the entire ships manifest had been slaughtered. The company came to the costly conclusion that putting psychopaths and sociopaths together in a confined space with large dangerous mining equipment was not such a great idea.

That is where Devon McAdams came in. He had hacked into his first computer at the age of seven and had been expelled from multiple schools. He was somewhat of a legend on the dark web when he discovered a weakness in the Alisa block chain which had been touted as unhackable. But he knew, as hackers did, that all software is written by humans and therefore always subject to human error. He went on to work as a freelance computer hacker on the dark web and, for a price, he could make people disappear or create entirely new identities. He'd never found a databank he couldn't hack into.

The Turn Corporation had flown him to capital city of Astana two years ago, having paid him an obscene amount of money to perform what they called *computer procurement*. Essentially, his job was to hack into the databases of the neo-Eastern Bloc State prison system looking for appropriate candidates who could be pressed into service. For example, he could take a healthy 25-year-old soccer player who was imprisoned for game fixing and with a couple of hours work; the soccer player would have a new identity as a serial killer. The perfect person for impressment into the ships mining contingency. This was the type of prison system where it was not unusual for inmates to disappear. Any pangs of guilt Devon felt had been deadened by the large monthly injections of cash. He found it easier just not to think about the lives he was destroying.

The last piece of the puzzle to be placed was when he saw a crate with the word TEMNO stenciled on its side.

Oh crap, fuck me running. The Temno was the newest of the Turn Corporation's deep space mining fleet.

"How long?" he barked at Doc.

"About 19 years. Our med team ferried over from the Zhel to start the activation process. Our ore holds are almost full and we will be heading home in a few months. The crew was awakened about two weeks ago and now it is time for you to go over the systems before we bring the rest of the miners out of stasis."

"But why? I was doing great work for the Turn Corporation. Why was I impressed for this mission?"

The doctor paused as he turned from his computer screen to look at Devon.

"Everyone needs a good IT guy."

THE DRAIN

"OW" HE YELLED. A ROUGH AREA ON HIS FINGERNAIL HAD caught in the loose fibers of his nylon backpack. It was a cheap brand and he was always snagging things on it.

"Oh, you big baby," quipped Matthew, his eight year old brother. He and his bother Lawrence, who was eleven, had just moved into the town of Oak City. A new school waited for them and like many times in the past, they were going to be the 'new kids'. Their family moved around a lot due to their father's job, which was setting up water treatment plants for small towns when they changed over from well water systems to reservoir systems.

They both put on their backpacks and walked out the front door toward the school. They lived about one mile from the school and they walked past a large flood plain that bordered the housing addition. On the opposite side of the flood plain they could see a large drainage ditch that ran out from a gapping concrete drain looked like a giant mouth in the side of the hill that made up the east side of the flood plain. They both stared at the opening and a chill ran down Lawrence's spine though he did not know why.

"Looks like a big old mouth, huh," said Matthew. "Kinda spooky".

"Yeah," Lawrence answered. "Kinda spooky." Another chill ran down his spine and he noticed goose bumps standing up on his arms.

At school they split up and went to their separate class rooms. They spent the rest of the day going thru the awkward stages of getting to know the school, the teachers and kids. Lawrence was the shy one and tended to stand at the edge of life as an observer whereas Matthew would jump in and would have five friends by the end of the day.

At lunch, Lawrence was sitting with three boys who were talking about playing ball. It seemed that the new water treatment plant was being built on the old playground and they were without a field to play ball.

"What about the flood plain," inquired Lawrence? "It would make a great place to play."

All three boys stopped talking and stared at Lawrence and he immediately knew he had said something wrong. They all had a look of fear in their eyes and he thought his saw one of them shiver. They tallest one said, "Look, kid. You are new here so let me say this once and only once. Don't ever go on the plain. Not for a second. Don't even think about it."

"But why? Why can't we go play in the field?"

"Because," he said, his eyes becoming small and his voice soft,

"There is a monster living in the drain."

"Oh sure" Lawrence snapped back. He had the feeling that they were making fun of him and he could feel himself getting defensive with a knot in his stomach. He could feel their eyes on him and kept expecting them to break into a laugh or smile or something. But, they just continued to stare at him with a look of terror that he slowly realized was not an act.

The two smaller kids were looking around nervously as if they were being called into the principals' office. The taller kid continued. "About five years ago they put in that drain and from what I've been told they found some old caves that went back for miles into the side of the hill. Then two years ago people starting missing their pets, like cats and dogs. And last year a three year old girl disappeared. They never found any sign of her." The recess bell rang and they started back to the classroom.

At the end of the day, the tall kid handed him a note. 'Stay away from the drain' was all it said.

That night Lawrence told Matthew what he had heard in school. Matthew didn't believe it and thought the kids were just playing joke on him.

Matthew was like that. He never believed anything he was told and always demanded to prove things for himself. He was a true "doubting Thomas' in miniature form.

"I don't know Matt. You didn't see the look on their faces. If they were acting, then they were doing a good job of it."

At that moment, a little black fur ball came running up. This was Nikki, their little black poodle that was the family dog but spent most of her time with Matthew and Lawrence. They traded off letting her sleep in their beds much to the dislike of their mother who felt that dogs germs would surely give them some strangely exotic disease. She was always worrying about things like that. Nikki jumped up on the bed with a jingle that came from her dog tags on her red collar.

The next day, as they were walking to school, Nikki walked with them. As passed in front of the drain opening Nikki started growling deeply and the hairs were standing up on the back of her neck. This was very unusual as Nikki was the friendliest dog in the world. She had grown up with two boys and had been mauled, stepped on, dressed up and put thru many humiliations, all with a willing spirit. But today Matthew and Lawrence heard a new sound from her. A sound that dogs had been making since they first entered into the firelight with ancient man. A sound that spoke of a great terror in the darkness. A sound of warning.

Matthew and Lawrence nervously exchanged glances but said nothing as they walked on to the school in silence.

On Friday, it was Matthews turn to feed Nikki and he called to her but she did not come. This was strange for Nikki never missed a meal as you could tell by her fat little butterball shape. Matthew called to her again and he thought he heard a high pitch yelp far off in the distance. Lawrence came out the back door and asked what was going on. Matthew explained that Nikki had not come home for dinner and he had heard a dog cry out somewhere towards the field.

They started walking towards the flood plain, calling out her name every few minutes. Lawrence caught sight of some small footprints in the mud at the bottom of the ditch that ran from the large drain. The footprints lead into the drain. Matthew started into the drain and Lawrence grabbed his shoulder.

"You can't go in there."

"Get your hand off of me. If Nikki is in there then I'm going after her." Matthew said defiantly.

"But it is getting dark and besides, it is not safe."

"What do you mean 'not safe'? You don't believe all that stuff you heard about monsters do you?"

Lawrence dodged the question and replied, "Well, its getting dark and we don't have any flashlights."

"Oh, OK. But I'm coming back in the morning and I'm going into the drain." Matthew said with determination.

The next morning was Saturday and Matthew was up early packing his bag. He put in a ball of string, a sling shot and a jug of water. He strapped on a small knife that he wore on his hip. It was an old knife that had a bone handle and a six-inch blade. It had been given to him by his father who had made it when he was younger. Matt's father had always been allowed to have knives at a young age and although it drove his mom nuts, he was trusted with the knife as long as he treated it with respect. Matthew liked knives and kept the edge very sharp. There were many things that Matthew was sloppy about but this was not one of them. He prided himself on how he took care of his knives.

Lawrence watched as Matthew packed. His Dad was away on the construction site and wouldn't be back until Monday. If he said anything to his Mother, then she would just tell them not to go and that might be too late for Nikki. He couldn't let his brother go by himself because even for all their fighting over a million little things, he knew that it was his duty as the older brother to watch out after the younger. The family had many unwritten laws and one of them was that of loyalty to each other.

Lawrence collected some matches, a candle, and a hammer that he got from the toolbox. He put these with four peanut butter sandwiches in his own backpack. They both had their scouting flashlights, which they clipped on to their belts.

"You know we shouldn't be doing this. We should wait for Dad," Lawrence tried to reason logically.

Logic was not something that Matthew accepted easily. He was pure emotion and energy and often got into trouble because he did things without thinking. Lawrence was cautious to the point of sometimes being fearful. They were both so different but like the moon that has a dark and light side, they were connected by the bond of birth. The bond of brotherhood whose depth neither would appreciate until they were much older.

"You don't have to come," Matthew replied although in his eyes there was a touch of fear that Lawrence might change his mind and abandon him. He would never admit it until he was much older, just how much he looked up to his older brother and often acted at his worst when he wanted to get Lawrence's attention.

"I'm coming. I'm coming," Lawrence said. He could hear in his mind one of the million lectures that his Dad was known for giving. The one he was replaying now was about the importance of sticking together and watching out for each other. Dads' main form of education was in the form of stories, lectures and long dissertations about philosophies of life.

They walked down the street until they reached the ditch that ran back to opening of the drain. In was about 10 am and the sun was just heating up the late May sky. They could smell the drying slime and mud that lined the bottom of the ditch. They jumped lightly from dry spot to dry spot like a long rotting hopscotch game. As they got closer to the drain they could now see they the opening was covered by a large rusting grate. The grate was firmly attached to the sides by large bolts. Matthew tugged at it but it did not budge.

"Well, I guess we can't go in," Lawrence said trying to sound disappointed though secretly relieved.

"Look how wide these bars are. I bet we can squeeze through them," Matthew answered. And to prove his point he took off his back pack and easily worked himself into the drain. "Come on. You can do it."

Lawrence took off his pack and handed it to Matthew through the bars. Then he put his arm and leg through. It was much tighter and he was afraid that he might get stuck.

"Come on. Suck it in." Matthew encouraged.

Lawrence pulled in his stomach and by rocking back and forth finally got through. They were in the drain. They noticed immediately that there was a coolness in the air like the end of autumn. And there was a breeze that could be felt and carried in the breeze was a stink like rotting fish washed on the shore. It was the smell of decay. It was the smell of death. Suddenly they felt trapped and both had the urge to get out of the drain, to get back through the bars into the safety of the light.

Matthew turned on his flashlight and took a step into the darkness. Lawrence said, "I'll go first." And to his surprise Matthew didn't fight or argue with him. At that moment, Lawrence knew Matthew was scared too but that his pride would never let him admit it.

They slowly began to walk into the darkness. They could feel the soft mud as it squished under their feet. They walked around they piles of old twisted brush and collections of debris from countless rainstorms. They saw a kid's tennis shoe.

"Some kid must have lost it during a rain storm." Matthew quietly stated.

"Yeah, I guess so," Lawrence answered although he was thinking of the missing girl that he had been told about in school.

They walked further and further into the drain. The comfort of the opening was getting dimmer with each step. And with each step their hearts began to beat faster. They could feel they flashlight getting slippery in their hands due the sweat of their palms.

"Nikki," Matthew called.

"Auugh," Lawrence screamed. "Jesus, Matthew, you scared me half to death", Lawrence had almost forgotten why they were on this journey.

As they continued to walk, they noticed there was water seeping from the walls and suddenly the concrete ended and natural rock formations started. This must have been the place where the construction had broken into a set of natural caves. Caves that had been undisturbed for thousands of years. Caves that once were linked to the surface

"This is far enough," Lawrence said. "If we haven't found Nikki by now, then we won't."

"You are probably right." Matthew said reluctantly. As they started to leave, they both heard it at the same time. It was very faint but very distinct. It was the jingle of dog tags that they knew very well. "It's Nikki. It sounds like she is right behind that pile of rocks. Nikki. Come on Nikki. Here girl."

They walked over to a large pile of rubble that was at the opening to another tunnel. The smell of putrid decay was stronger. Matthew stumbled over something and almost fell. Lawrence aimed his light down at what had tripped his brother. It looked like the floor was littered with sticks but his stomach turned and he gasped as he realized that they were bones. Piles and piles of bones. And skulls. Large and small. Some animals he recognized. Some were unfamiliar.

"Matthew. We got to get out of here. Now." Lawrence almost screamed.

"There's Nikki," Matthew said, as he caught sight of a pile of black fur with a red collar. The dog tags were moving gently in the ever present breeze of the cave.

Matthew reached over to pick up Nikki.

"Yaaaahhh," he screamed at the top of his lungs. A pile a matted bloodied fur came away in his hand. A leg was hanging by threads of torn flesh. Matthew screamed again as he threw it down in disgust.

They both turned to run when a sound stopped them. A deep rumbling sound like a thousand angry wolves. It was coming from behind them. They turned and shown their flashlights but all they saw were hints of movement. Now it was to their right. And then to their left. They turned wildly trying to put the light on whatever was making that sound. The rumbling grew louder as all the growls become one. One unholy note that reverberated off the walls. A sound that spoke of terror, of pain, of hatred. They felt the ground vibrate under the footsteps of some beast. Some beast that had been trapped for eons in the depths of the cave only to be freed by the construction five years ago. An ancient beast, a monster that waited in the dark for the unwary animal that came into the drain to get out of the heat of the sun or a snowstorm. Or maybe the small child who was unfortunate enough to wander off from their family.

And now it was coming for them. They were frozen like the stalactites that littered the floor of the cave that was to become their tomb. Like a bubble of methane gas that rises from the muck of a swamp, a tiny sound began deep in Lawrence's chest and gained speed as it rushed to the surface. It broke loose with a loud "Run."

They began to run not caring where they stepped. Not caring that mud mixed with bits of pieces of rotting flesh and hair of past kills was splattering on to their clothes, their face, their hands. They tried not to think of what was splashing into their mouths as they spit out unthinkable filth with revulsion.

Lawrence was in the lead and they were nearing the grate. The doorway to the light. The portal of their freedom. He could hear the footsteps getting closer and heard the sound of claws as they scrapped along the walls and floor. He could hear the labored breathing of some beast as the growls grew louder as the monster closed in on its prey. "They were going to die," he thought. "Going to die in some stupid drain, in some stupid little town'"

He was almost to the grate when he heard a thump and a cry. '"Lawrence, help me."

He turned and in the light of Matthews's flashlight, he saw that Matthew had slipped in the mud. Matthews hand was reaching up to Lawrence and his face was twisted in terror and fear.

"Lawrence, Help," he pleaded again. Lawrence looked at the grate, the light and could smell the clean air of safety. But without hesitation he turned and headed back into the drain, back into the darkness. He had no choice. It was his brother.

Lawrence ran back to where Matthew had fallen and quickly helped him up and half pushing, half carrying him he threw Matthew in front of him. Together they ran to the light, to the opening of the drain. Lawrence could feel the presence of the monster as it rapidly gained on the boys.

Matthew reached the grate and threw himself between the bars and began to run. Lawrence dared a glance over his shoulder and saw a large lumbering shape closing in on him. He could see the light shining back from two large red eyes. He got the impression of long arms that almost touched the floor. He turned back and began to wedge himself thru the bars of the grate.

Matthew, now free of the drain and on solid ground, ran, pumping his legs, putting all his strength into getting away from the drain.

Lawrence was almost thru. He could feel the warmth of the sun on his face. His heart almost exploded with joy as he freed himself from the grate.

A cry of relief was in his throat when suddenly he felt himself being lifted up and was slammed against the bars. A long hideous and disfigured arm had snaked out between the bars like a striking viper and had sunk its claws into the pack that was still on his back. His head slammed against the metal bars. A stabbing pain shot through his head. He bit his tongue and could taste the salty wetness of his own blood. He was dazed and he was afraid he was going to pass out. He was being shaken as the monster tried to pull him back through the bars. He heard it bellow in rage as it was frustrated by having its prey within its reach but being unable to finish the kill. Lawrence felt its other arm come between the bars and start to close in on his chest, crushing him against the grate.

He then saw a flash of color as Matthew leaped up and drove his knife into stinking gnarled arm of the beast. The monster let of a roar as if it were calling to all the demons of hell. It tried to pull back its arm but the claws of the arm that had grabbed Lawrence first, had snagged in the nylon of his old backpack. Matthew stabbed into the darkness behind Lawrence where he could only see the swirling of shapes. The knife struck again and he felt it go deep and slide along bone. Again, the monster cried out in pain and rage and tore his claws from the nylon trap with one mighty effort.

Lawrence was snapped forward like a rubber band and fell hard on his face. The air was knocked out of his lungs. He felt Matthew grab him as they both struggled to their feet. They ran and did not stop running until they reached the safety of their own bedroom.

They collapsed on the floor each gasping for breath and threw off their packs. After a moment, they looked at each other and half crying and half laughing hugged each until it became awkward. They let go of each other as their breathing slowly returned to normal

The police and hunters took off the grate and explored the drain but they didn't find anything but the bones and fur and Nikki's collar. There had been a thunderstorm that night and by the time they got to the drain the next day, all the tracks and signs of the struggle had been washed away under cleansing waters.

There was talk that a wild dog or even rabid wolf had chased the boys. No one believed the story of the monster. No one except the children of Oak City. The adults did close the drain with explosives so maybe that showed they believed more than they were willing to admit.

Summer came and went and once again, they were packing up to move to another city, for another job. As Lawrence and Matthew were boxing up their toys, they talked of the new town. They didn't talk much about what happened in the drain and sometimes it almost seemed as if was just a dream and sometimes they wondered if it had really happened at all. Was it just a child's imagination playing tricks on them in the dark? Did their own fears just come to life and become real enough to scare them? Was it just a lost trapped dog that had chased them? These are the thoughts that haunted them as they worked in silence together on that late summer's day.

Matthew reached behind the toy box and pulled out Lawrence's back pack that had been thrown there and forgotten months ago after they had returned from the drain.

"Lawrence," Matthew called almost in a hush.

Lawrence didn't look up and said, "What?"

"Lawrence, look." Matthew said with an intensity that caught Lawrence's attention. Lawrence looked to where Matthew was standing and saw him holding his old backpack. It was torn and tattered but then Lawrence saw it. Stuck in a tangle of nylon fibers with a bit of dried tendon still clinging to it was a four-inch claw.

THE LAST SHALL BE FIRST

THE FOG WAS GETTING THICKER, HE THOUGHT, CONCEN-trating on the rhythmic slap of his feet as they made contact with the pavement. This was his third marathon since moving to San Francisco and, other than the fog; it was a perfect morning for running. Cool but not cold. He focused on the number 413 pinned to the shirt of the runner in front of him. Number 413 had been in the lead since the beginning of the race and he was contemplating making his move at the next leg of the race.

The number was becoming more indistinct, and he blinked to try to clear the morning mist from his eyes. The lead runner appeared to be fading into the morning fog and he could see outlines of other objects through the form of runner 413. As his mind was trying to comprehend what he was seeing, the runner faded into nothingness. He stopped to find the clothing strewn on the ground, number 413 flapping in the gentle morning breeze.

* * *

AKIO AND HITOMI HELD HANDS AS THEY WALKED HOME from their school located in the outskirts of Tokyo. They giggled and laughed and sometimes spoke in hushed tones as they discussed the events of the day. Akio was watching their hands swinging back and forth when she saw the hand of her friend beginning to disappear. She gasped. Within seconds, her gasp changed to a scream of horror and disbelief as she turned to watch her friend vanish from sight, leaving behind a rumpled piled clothing.

This is how it began.

* * *

BOONE MONTGOMERY TRIED TO MASSAGE AWAY THE DULL ache throbbing in his temples. For three tedious hours he'd been at a computer terminal trying to complete his assigned lessons under the urgings of his tutor, Mary. She was a soft-spoken graduate student whose job was to encourage him in his studies, but the intensity of her urgings often became somewhat tiresome causing him tune her out. Her hair flowed long over her shoulders; it shine and color reminded him of the minks they sometimes trapped back home. His adolescent attention was easily distracted by the curve of her neckline, a subtle scent of her perfume, or the touch of her hand on his shoulder as she tried to explain a new mathematical concept to him. Like everyone else at the university, she was driven by the intense desire to make the last months, years, or even minutes of her life meaningful.

When Boone was younger, he and his sister liked to play with the toy called Hot Potato, a wind-up device with a timer that was set to go off at random intervals. The object of the game was to toss the toy to another child and not have it in your possession when time ran out and it exploded. He often wondered if this is how the rest of the world felt, wondering if today was the day the potato would explode.

Until a year ago, he'd never seen a computer, and now it had become his life. He didn't like the feeling that the fate of the world was on his shoulders. Although, in his case, this wasn't an exaggeration.

"That's enough for now. You look tired. Let's take a thirty minute break and try to get in one more good session before dinner," Mary said in a soothing, somewhat sexy voice that always had undertones of sadness. "I hear there's fresh banana bread in the cafeteria."

"Great," replied Boone. "I'm also going to stop by the clinic to see if I can get something for this headache. I'll meet you back here in half an hour."

She smiled at him as he left, and he felt himself blush despite having learned not to become attached to the various tutors he had while at the university.

As he sat in the cafeteria, munching on the still warm banana bread, his mind wandered back to the first few days after he had arrived at the University. He hadn't asked to be selected, and at first he'd resented being taken away from his family. Although, if he were asked to logically examine the situation, he would be forced to agree with the decision.

It had been fifty years since the discovery and development of tele-transportation. A group of scientists who'd grown up watching Kirk and the crew of the Enterprise using the transporter had finally discovered the technology that would allow movement of organic and inorganic matter through space by way of stabilized wormholes. The discovery had changed almost every aspect of the world's society overnight. Every home and business had a port. This essentially brought about the total collapse of the trucking, automotive, rail, the airlines and shipping industries. If a family couldn't afford a porting unit, they could simply walk to the corner bus stop, which had been replaced by porting units.

Cruise lines remained viable as people still enjoyed the relaxation of slowly going from point A to point B. There were still many car enthusiasts and those who liked to fly who maintained their precious relics from the past. And, there were a few factories still capable of producing ground and air transportation, though they were mostly geared up for sports and recreational vehicles.

The system was quite simple. A person would approach a porting station, swipe their personal ID card and, after funding was approved, they would key in their destination, walk through the portal and find themselves at the local shopping mall or their dentist's office. Larger portals allowed for the transportation of cargo between manufacturers and retailers.

It was calculated that over 99.5% of the world's population had used a port at least once. Only the most primitive or eccentric cultures did not use porting. From the day a baby left the hospital in its mother's arms and was ported to their home, porting was woven into the fabric of everyday life.

Boone's family was one of the unconventional exceptions. They had been part of the doomsday movement and had moved to the Appalachian Mountains of eastern Kentucky in the early part of the 21st Century. He'd been born at home by a midwife into a small community of survivalists who feared the world was on the edge of destruction. Diseases, nuclear attack and foreign invasion, were all eventualities the community anticipated. They prided themselves on their ability to thrive without modern technology.

A product of home schooling, Boone had just finished the equivalent of the 10th grade. From his father and other members of the compound, he was taught how to fix and maintain the basic equipment which helped the compound to thrive. He learned how to repair and rebuild the generators and other essential machinery which provided power for the water pump and other simple electrical needs. He mastered the skills to work on the ATV's and the old military trucks which had been converted to run on bio-diesel fuel. His life had been simple and uncomplicated until the day of the Big Flare.

Before the day of the Big Flare, the largest solar flare ever recorded had been the Carrington event on September 1, 1859. Although massive, effects on the world were minimal as the technology of the day was somewhat primitive. The only noticeable problem recorded was the increase in static and disruptions of telegraph services. The Big Flare was measured to be twice as large as the Carrington event and had released massive amounts of radiation across the electromagnetic spectrum at all wavelengths, from radio waves to gamma rays. This event produced the first clear evidence of several new spectral components above 200 GHz.

There were massive world-wide blackouts. Countries, governments and economies were in a state of panicked chaos until the power was restored over a period of several weeks. The world slowly returned to normal and as far as any scientists could tell, no long-term harm had been done. But they were wrong.

The Fades were sporadic isolated events and were originally written off by authorities as kidnappings or runaways. But then reports started coming in from all over the world of people spontaneously fading out of existence. Still, there was little concern and murmurs of mass hallucinations were the explanation of the day, until Eva Cruz, a popular actress from the top running television Hispanic show *Sin Tetas No Hay Paraíso*, faded during the taping of the show. The video went viral on the Internet and there were enough in person witnesses that the world authorities started asking for answers.

Unfortunately, the answer was horrific in its scale. Massive outbursts of previously unknown radiation frequencies of the Big Flare had flooded the world. This had the unexpected effect of destabilizing the molecular bonds which held together all organic material. Any living creature that had ever passed through a tele-transportation unit was at risk of having its molecules released from its bonds and simply dispersed into space. It didn't matter if a person had ported one time or one thousand times; the risk was the same and was ruthlessly random.

At first people tried to fight the Fade. They tried living in lead shielded boxes, moving to the mountains and living in the deepest mine tunnels. They tried putting restraints on their children as they slept, only to find empty tethers in the morning. Mothers collapsed in unbearable sorrow when babies disappeared while nursing at their breasts. The world's population was being decimated and there was nothing anyone could do to slow or alter the process.

Initially, there were worldwide panics and riots, until the inevitability of what was happening finally took hold of society's consciousness.

The world's focus dramatically and swiftly changed from survival of the masses to the survival of species. Every country rushed to find groups of people who had never used the porting system. The plan was to find young people who could be taught to preserve the basic culture. They would then be given crash courses in what were considered to be the basic survival skills such as medicine, engineering, agriculture and construction. It was felt that if the population could have the basic technology that existed in 1930, it would have a reasonable chance to survive and to eventually once again flourish.

The first concern was child care. Once the side effect of porting was discovered, newborn infants were no longer transported home. There was a rush to find antique cars and trucks, which were converted into makeshift ambulances to carry home these fragile hopes of the world's future. Because it was impossible to predict when an infant's parents would fade, early on, there had been many infant deaths as newborns had been left orphaned and unattended. The reality was, the risk of losing a newborn to unintended abandonment was too great. Laws were passed ensuring all newborns would be taken into protective custody and sent to regional centers to be cared for, as it was impossible to predict when an infant's parents might fade. This also necessitated a declaration of martial law.

Overnight, the destitute, the shunned, the homeless, all of society's castaways were sought after to be nurtured, educated and groomed to be the caretakers of the new world. All of the world's governments began pouring resources into the rapid training and education of those previously discarded classes. Brazil swept up almost 1,000,000 street children for their reeducation efforts. China found children and young adults in its most rural provinces. Industrialized countries such a Sweden and Norway imported children and young adults from the slums of New Delhi. The United States was in negotiation with the elders of the Amish community, but had yet been able to convince them that recent events were anything more than "Gods will" which should be allowed to play out.

One of the most sought after groups were Tibetan monks. They had never accepted the concept of porting as they felt it would interfere with the reincarnation of their souls. Their beliefs that the journey was as important as the destination meant they had continued to travel using technology that predated porting. The University was lucky in that there were three monks working with the program. They helped provide continuity as it was impossible to predict when a member of the governance board would fade.

Boone and his younger sister, Tilly, had been brought to the campus of George Washington University where they were housed in the dorms with thousands of other adolescents and young adults. Tilly, at age 13, was involved in a pediatric nursing program with the ultimate goal of training her to be a pediatrician, if there was enough time. Part of her daily training involved learning to care for the hundreds of infants who occupied several floors of the University's hospital.

Boone's aptitude test placed him in the training path of a mechanical/electrical engineer.

* * *

BOONE DECIDED HE NEEDED A SECOND PIECE OF BANANA bread and some cold milk to wash it down. Although the cafeteria was crowded with a mix of adults and young people, as well as military personnel in a traditional green camouflage uniforms, he sat alone as he often did on his breaks.

He recalled his early days at the University. In the beginning, Boone had planned to escape from the facilities with the goal of returning home. Everything around him made him feel stupid: the faculty, the older students, and the technology. He felt out of place, and the deep loneliness he felt caused him to ache for the hills of eastern Kentucky. But he would never leave without his sister, and Tilly was having what she felt to be an unimaginable adventure. Every night she would almost glow and sparkle as she shared with him all she had learned that day in class.

Boone remembered the day in the break room when he was sitting alone, feeling very lost and empty. He'd felt a presence behind him and turned to find one of the Tibetan monks, draped in red robe, standing behind him with a cup of tea. He had learned that the color of the monks' robes often indicated where they were from. Red signifying Tibet, saffron from India and brown from Thailand.

The monk had asked permission to sit with him, something Boone had reluctantly agreed to. They sat in silence for several minutes. Boone watched the monk slowly and deliberately, stir his hot tea. The scent of jasmine, with just a hint of cinnamon, reached Boone.

"We are both on a journey which neither asked for nor expected." The monk spoke as if talking to no one in particular. "But such is the nature of life, unexpected roads to unknown destinations. Each person trying to find their own way."

He stopped and slowly, with purpose, sipped his tea.

"It is our belief that all human suffering arises from misunderstanding the nature of the world. Unfortunately, the present state has sadly proven this to be true." He paused, before continuing. "Would you walk with me?"

Without comment, the Tibetan monk stood and walked to the door. Boone hesitated for only a second before following him out of the break room. In silence, they walked to a series of classrooms which had been converted into newborn nurseries. Sounds of babies crying echoed through the hallways. He stopped and opened up the door of one of the converted nurseries where Boone could see Tilly, listening attentively to a nurse talking about the importance of infant nutrition. She was accompanied by two other adolescent females from a distant Navajo reservation in New Mexico.

After a few moments, the monk spoke. "These are the seeds of the future and this," he said gesturing to the room, "is the garden. Young souls, like you and your sister, have been chosen by destiny to be the gardeners. The task that has been laid upon you is to nurture and care for the future of the world. To lead, to teach, to protect."

"To protect?" These were the first words Boone had spoken since leaving the cafeteria.

For the first time, the monk made direct eye contact Boone.

"Yes, Mister Boone. Sadly, history has shown us that when resources become scarce, the dark side of human nature appears. Even though you're being trained as an engineer, you will also receive training in self-defense and weapons as befits your role as protector."

As Boone's eyes scanned the bassinets, he began to notice their individual differences. In the past, his adolescent maleness had perceived all babies as being the same. Tiny things that cried, smelled bad, and should be avoided at all costs. Their skin colors ranged from the darkest black to the palest pink, but they all had one thing in common, they were helpless and they needed him. A previously undeveloped part of his personality was awakening like a sleeping dragon, that of defender.

He and the monk both watched the infants for several moments. Some were sleeping, some were making gurgling baby sounds and some were whimpering trying to decide if they should cry.

"A philosopher, Francis Bacon is credited to have said 'Knowledge Is Power'. This is going to be never more true than in the days and years to come." He paused, taking a last look at the infants. "Thank you for walking with me, Mr. Boone." With that, the monk turned and walked away.

Boone suddenly felt as if the future of the world had been laid upon his shoulders. He inhaled a large breath, held it for a second, and then let go a long sigh. With the sigh he said farewell to the innocence of youth and the irresponsibility of adolescence. He accepted the heavy cloak of adulthood and remembered one of the stories his mother had taught him from the Bible. He now understood what Jesus meant when he said: 'Father, if you are willing, take this cup away from me. Yet not my will but yours be done.'

Standing alone in the hallway, he wondered if he should have paid more attention to his mother's lessons.

* * *

THE LARGE CRASH OF A DROPPED A SERVING TRAY JOLTED Boone's wondering attention from memories back to the present. As he finished his snack before heading back to class, he thought about how much his life had changed since the day he'd met the monk in the cafeteria. He had later found out that the monks name was Master Kunchen, which translated to 'all knowing'. He remembered smiling at this revelation.

Boone returned to the classroom and was surprised to find that his tutor, Mary, was not there. In all the months they had worked together, she'd never been late for session. He sat down at his computer and opened up the math program he'd been working on before the break. He was assured that mathematics would become the foundation of everything to follow in his accelerated curriculum of engineering.

He looked up when he heard the door open. In walked an older woman he recognized as one of the professors of the engineering department.

"Where is Mary? She's..." He stopped as he saw tears well up in the older woman's eyes.

"Mary," she said trying hard to maintain her composure, "my daughter, is gone."

They looked at each other for several seconds until the awkwardness of direct eye contact forced them to turn away.

"I am so sorry," said Boone as he turned back to the computer screen.

"Thank you."

She walked behind Boone and placed her hand on his shoulder and with a catch in her voice said, "Now Mr. Montgomery, where did Mary leave off?"

THE POST CARD

I LOOKED AT THE POST CARD IN MY HAND, WITH ITS PICTURE of an idyllic beach surrounded by tall swaying palm trees. As I held the card, I swore I could smell the salt breeze and hear the surf crashing on the beach. I turned it over and saw that the sender was from my patient Kyla. As I looked at the card, I was taken back to our last visit.

It was a fall Monday afternoon; Oklahoma was just beginning to cool down and the excitement of college football was in the air. I knocked on the door of the exam room, waited a few seconds and then walked into the exam room while scanning Kyla's chart. The last time she'd been in was almost a year ago when it had been time for her annual exam. I'd been her doctor for over 20 years, having first seen her when she was 18 years old. I was just starting practice and was green, straight out of residency. I'd delivered both of her children and developed a warm fondness for her that I reserved for special patients. I always looked forward to seeing her and being able to catch up on her life and her family.

"So, Kyla, what's going on exciting in your world?" I asked with my usual opening line.

She didn't say anything. I looked up from my chart to see she was sitting with her head bowed, almost as if in prayer, with a wad of Kleenex in her hands. I quickly put down the chart and touched her knee slightly with my hand and asked what was wrong.

"I guess you don't watch the news?" she said cryptically.

"I don't," I acknowledged and waited for her to say more.

Her story unfolded as she explained that the prior Wednesday evening, she was at the public library as a volunteer and helping teach English as a second language to foreign nationals. Without warning, the police interrupted her class and took her outside. They explained they had just arrested her husband on charges of trying to hire someone to murder her. The officer told her that her husband had offered an undercover decoy $10,000 to carry out the murder. At first, she couldn't believe what she'd heard. It wasn't until she saw the body cam video of her husband planning the details of her death that she became convinced.

It didn't make sense. Her husband was a firefighter, a deacon in her church and they had been faithfully married for over 20 years.

"I am so sorry, Kyla. You must feel awful. I don't—"

"Oh, there's more," she interrupted.

My eyebrows rose in anticipation. "More?"

"Yes. Saturday night he hung himself in his cell."

I was stunned. In less than a week, Kyla had gone from a happily married wife to having her world destroyed by the knowledge her husband had tried to have her killed and then suddenly becoming a widow.

"Kyla, I don't know what to say. This is something out of a TV crime show." I paused, then added, "We really don't have to do this exam today. We can reschedule it for some time in the future. You have much more important things to deal with than your annual exam."

"I know," she said staring intently at me, as a stray tear ran down her cheek making a mascara stream. "But today I need something normal and, after 20 years of coming here, this feels normal. Also, I need your medical advice about something. Something I don't understand."

"Okay." I paused, letting the word hang there until she was ready to speak.

"Do you know anything about magic or mind control?"

He leaned back in surprise. "What do you mean?"

"Well, they let me talk to my husband, Jeff, after he was arrested. I begged him for an explanation, but what he told me didn't make any sense. It sounded crazy." With her Kleenex she caught another stray tear winding itself down her cheek.

"He said that while on a church sponsored mission trip to Costa Rica, they'd traveled to a village where they'd been told there was an actively practicing witch. The leaders of the mission trip felt this was a perfect opportunity to evangelize to the village and to remove the control the witch had over them." She paused. "May I have a drink of water?"

I pushed a button which let the nurse know I needed her. When she arrived, I explained our need and she quickly brought in a cup of water for Kyla.

She sipped her water slowly, and then continued with her story.

"He said when he entered into her house, what he found was totally unexpected. He'd prepared himself for an old, snaggletooth hag, but what he found was a beautiful dark-haired woman who looked to be in her early twenties. She said her name was Ayesha. What really took him by surprise, were her eyes. He said they had a strange emerald luminescence and seemed to glow in the dim light of her home. He felt drawn to her and when she reached out her hand, he took it. As soon as they touched, he knew he had found his truelove, his soul mate."

Kyla began to sob, and I allowed her a few minutes to work through the pain of discussing her husband's illicit love affair.

"I know this must be very difficult for you to discuss."

"It's just that I have to get the story out. I have got to tell this to someone, someone I trust."

She took a deep sigh, composed herself and continued.

"He said when he was with Ayesha he felt a limitless love that was surreal and reminded him of psychedelic mushroom trips he used to take when he was younger. He didn't even question her when she suggested he return to the United States, arrange for my death and then returned to Costa Rica with the insurance money." Kayla now had a bit of spite and anger in voice which I felt was healthy. "Their plan was to build a tourist resort on the coast and to live happily ever after."

"So, Doc, what do you think? Do you think she put some type of spell on him? Some type of witch doctor voodoo? Some drug, some herb? And what do you make of her eyes?"

I didn't know what to think or to believe. I explained I really had nothing to offer on the subject, although I did believe there were things in this world that science couldn't find answers for.

"I think that after I settle the estate, I'm going down there to track the bitch down."

"Whoa. Let's slow down a little bit. I don't think it's a good idea to go flying down to a foreign country and try to track down some strange woman who may have plotted to have you killed."

"We'll see" she said in a flat monotone voice, laced with anger.

Nothing else was said for the rest of the exam about her situation. As she was getting ready to leave he said, "If there is anything I can do to help you get through this, please let me know.

"Thank you, I will," She gave him a quick hug and was gone.

* * *

HE HAD HEARD NO FURTHER WORD FROM HER UNTIL HE
received the card. As I held the postcard and began to read the note, she'd
written me, I would still swear I could smell the salt and hear the sea birds
as they glided over the beach.

Dear Dr. K.

I just wanted to drop you a line saying that I did track
down Ayesha. I know you suggested I not go, but I had to and
I'm so thankful I did. She is the most amazing woman and,
against all odds, I have fallen head over heels in love with her.
Crazy, huh? I cashed out my savings and we are now halfway
through the construction of a luxurious resort. I hope you can
come down because I would love to have you meet Ayesha. My
husband was right about her eyes. They are magical.

Love, Kyla

P.S. Ayesha added a little something to your postcard ☺

TIME BUBBLE

DR. CHATTERLING WAS STARING INTENTLY AT THE COMPUTER screen. He was taller than most of this species, standing at almost four feet. His skin was the color of bronze, and he had reddish-brown tufted hair on his cheeks and at the tops of his ears. The hair on his cheeks was trimmed in a manner that gave the impression of old time mutton chop sideburns. His eyes were large, dark, and luminous, much larger than those of the humans he worked with. He wore a long coat as was customary to keep his large bushy tail from interfering with his work.

His hands looked small in comparison to his large body, and his arms were shorter than one would have expected.

In the laboratory, there was much excitement among the scientists, who were almost an equal mixture of humans and Ch-ch-ch chi, as they called themselves. Ch-ch-ch chi meant people of the trees. Since most humans had a hard time speaking the language of the Chi, as the humans called them, in most cases the Chi learned to speak a form of English that sounded like someone talking with their teeth chattering due to severe cold.

Although there was great camaraderie between the species now, that had not always been the case. In the past, there were great wars when the two cultures clashed, but over the last thousand years, these two great cultures and races had learned to adapt to each other and live in relative harmony.

The evolutionary timeline of the Chi was a mystery to both human and Chi anthropologists alike. Human evolution could be traced from the first true mammals appearing 220 million years ago in the Triassic period, to the oldest known primate-like mammal species, the Plesiadapis, 65 million years ago. The ancestors of the Chi seemed to arrive out of nowhere approximately 50 million years ago with a single line of evolution unlike any other species. This mystery was reason for the excitement swirling around the lab.

With the discovery of faster than light particles in 2010, researchers had developed the technology that allowed them to send probes into the distant past. The only limiting factor for this technology was energy. The farther a probe was sent into the past, the more energy it required. On this day, they were sending a probe back 50 million years which required enough energy to power New York City for a year.

The probe was a very sophisticated computer mini-lab, designed to sample air, soil, and radiation, as well as perform another dozen functions. It had a panoramic camera to capture a 360-degree view of the probe's position. The scientists had programmed it to stay in the past only a few minutes to minimize the risk of time contamination, which was the theory that a small change in the past could have dramatic effects in the future. It was the first of several planned probes to be sent back to the past.

Dr. Scott Peck walked over to Dr. Chatterling and peered intently into the monitor displaying a large silver cylinder. This was the sending chamber, containing the probe at a site a mile away from the lab, in a shielded salt cavern 500 feet below the surface.

The idea of the experiment was relatively simple. The probe would be encased in a time bubble, sent back 50 million years and then, when the energy was turned off and the time bubble collapsed, the probe would return to its original position in time and space. The idea was simple, other than the fact it had never been performed before and no one was truly sure of what might happen. Theories ranged from the best case scenario of nothing, to catastrophic changes in the timeline. This experiment was not without controversy and therefore came with significant government oversight.

The location of the probe was chosen because geological records indicated the area of evolutionary interest was a salt cavern on the edge of a small inland sea 50 million years ago. It was the area where the earliest fossil remains of the Chi had been discovered.

Dr. Peck put his hand on the shoulder of his friend and colleague of 20 years, Dr. Chatterling.

"Well, this is it. We will soon make one of the greatest discoveries in the history of man or, just maybe, blow us all to hell," he said with a hint of humor as well as worry in his voice.

"Well my friend, at least we will go out together," replied Dr. Chatterling. They had met in a graduate program at MIT and had been close friends ever since. They'd spent many evenings at each other's homes, Dr. Peck with his ground dwelling and Dr. Chatterling with his traditionally elevated home on posts approximately 20-30 feet in the air. The ancestors of the Chi had been tree dwellers and even with their advanced evolution, they still felt more comfortable sleeping above the ground.

They both watched the computer count down, which would automatically collapse the time bubble and bring the probe back to this time and space. When the computer reached zero, there was a sound as if a motor were winding down. A brief flicker of lights followed. Then silence.

The data from the probe was then downloaded to various departments depending on specialty. After the download, technicians in biohazard suits would examine the probe, testing it for any unknown pathogens.

Dr. Chatterling and Dr. Peck would be part of the team examining the photos from the panoramic camera.

The pictures started to appear on their computer monitor. A hushed silence filled the room as they realized they were looking at plants that had not been seen on this earth for millions of years – a lush forest of palms, ferns, and ginkgo trees. Each picture indicated the probe had arrived in the late Eocene period. Then on frame 316 there was an image that would change history of the past and the future, forever.

There in frame 316, approximately five feet from the probe, was a small metal box with the dimensions of approximately one cubic foot.

"What the hell?" exclaimed Dr. Peck.

Dr. Chatterling was making a rasping sound, the Chi signal of distress and warning.

It was impossible, but there it was. A photograph from 50 million years ago showed an obviously machined box. There was no rational explanation. This was not an elaborate hoax or photographic glitch. They were looking at something defying logical explanation.

"We have got to get that box," Peck said.

"Ch-ch ches, we must," Dr. Chatterling replied, losing command of the English language in his excitement.

Dr. Peck could see movement under his friend's coat, indicating his tail was flicking with excitement.

The next weeks were filled with multiple meetings and countless committees to discuss the implications of photo frame 316. Some of the officials still thought it must be an elaborate hoax, while others were scared of the implications, which generally revolved around the idea the box had to be an alien artifact. There was one thing everyone could agree on: an attempt to retrieve the box was of supreme importance.

The mathematicians and physicists worked around the clock to solve the problem of how to bring an item back from the past. There was no concern about time contamination since this artifact obviously did not belong in the Eocene period. The final solution involved increasing the power to the time bubble generator so it would enlarge to include the box and allow it to be picked up by the probe. Then, if the scientists were correct, when the time bubble collapsed, the box would be brought back into the present. This was all theoretical since it had never been attempted before.

A small reactor, originally designed for a nuclear aircraft carrier, was installed to provide the additional energy requirements for the next probe. The probe, itself, was redesigned to include a simple grappling arm and a storage bay where the metal box would be placed for retrieval. The probe's on-board computer was programmed with an optical sensor to scan the area, identify the metal box, and then place it into a holding container. The time bubble would then be collapsed and the probe, with its precious and mysterious cargo, would be brought back to the present time.

After months of testing, it was finally time for the main event. There were multiple diplomatic and government officials as well as an increase in the number of scientific personnel present. Although the test was kept under strict secrecy, rumors of the upcoming probe launch popped up across the internet.

Dr. Chatterling and Dr. Peck were sitting at the bank of computer screens showing the progression of events. There was a loud hum, which became louder as the small nuclear reactor powered up. The sound stopped abruptly and all of the indicators dropped to zero. The probe had been sent. Now, all they could do was wait.

After several minutes, there was once again a loud hum, a dimming of the lights, and then an abrupt silence indicating the probe had returned to its original time coordinates. Once again, men in sealed hazmat suits were the first to examine the probe. Through the televised link, they could watch what was happening with the large cylinder. After taking some initial readings, they then went to the collection chamber to see if the box had been retrieved.

A feeling of heavy excitement permeated the room as the two doctors opened the collection chamber. A collective gasp settled in the air from those who were watching the proceedings as the mysterious metal box came into view. It was placed in a sealed, airtight, clear box and taken to a negative pressure sealed lab for initial studies. All the studies would be done under the watchful eye of video cameras, to allow the other scientists to watch the procedures and provide input as needed.

The initial test was the optical scanning of the box from all angles with a high-resolution magnifying camera which revealed layer upon layer of dirt and dust from the years the box had been on the ground. Inside the box, they found a collection of small pellets about the size of grains of rice. As the camera zoomed in on the pellets, small fibers could be seen protruding from the surface of each.

Dr. Chatterling made a high pitch squeal and then said, "Those look like animal droppings."

"Shit," Dr. Peck said under his breath.

"Exactly."

As soon as the box and its contents were cleared for the risk of infection, the box was sent to the mechanical engineers for evaluation, and the biological content was sent for chemistry and DNA analysis.

The initial analysis of the box showed it was a stainless steel and titanium alloy, common materials in the military and space industries. One of the many findings, which could not be explained, was that carbon dating of the organic material showed the fecal droppings were from this time, not 50 million years in the past.

One theory was, the box indicated aliens had visited the world in the past and the box was trash they had left behind. Another popular theory was the box indicated there were parallel universes and somehow there had been a break between the two of these, which allowed intra dimensional contamination. There were some who believed this was an elaborate government hoax to foster funding of the time probe experiment.

Testing into the physical properties of the box was an ongoing process, taking weeks to complete. Meanwhile, other divisions proceeded with their time probe experiments. The next experimental step would be to send back in time two small mammalian creatures as test subjects, male and female, to identify if there were side effects to time travel. The chosen species was a member of the rodent family *Cavia porcellus*, the common guinea pig.

Dr. Chatterling and Dr. Peck's part of the probe process was the sending and the retrieving of the probes that were being developed in other parts of the research lab. Although, they had access to the ongoing research on the metal box, they were not intimately involved with the day-to-day details of that analysis. Most of the information was kept secret until it had been thoroughly analyzed and conclusions formulated. It was felt this would keep speculation and rumors to a minimum.

Dr. Chatterling was completing the final process before sending the test animals into the past. Dr. Peck was working in his office when he heard a knock on the door. In walked a short, stooped Chi in a white coat, with stitching on the breast pocket identifying him as Dr. Silvertree, head of the genetic analysis lab.

"Hey Scott, I just thought I would give you a heads-up on our final report which will be presented at the weekly conference meeting. As with everything associated with this box, the results are confusing. The fecal droppings gave us DNA most closely resembling the Chi which would lead us to believe, whatever was in the box, was an ancient ancestor of the Chi."

Dr. Silvertree paused as if he were deciding to say something else. After a few moments he said, "Lastly, we found a strand of human hair whose DNA was placed into the data bank and there is a match with one of the technicians working in the animal labs. He has been taken into custody for questioning but at this point, he's denying knowing anything about the box. Hell if we can figure out what all this means."

Dr. Silvertree's cell phone signaled an incoming call, and he waved goodbye as the left Dr. Peck's office.

Dr. Peck furrowed his brow as his mind tried to grasp what he'd just heard. A flicker of an idea came to him, but the thought was so absurd he quickly discounted it. However, the idea wouldn't go away, and he felt as if he had all the puzzle pieces before him. If only he could find the right combination to complete the picture.

He moved some papers on his desk until he found a diagram of the latest probe; the one designed to send two rodents back to the past and then retrieve them once again. In the center of the probe was an animal container with a latch designed to hold it securely. He then went to the photos to find a picture of the metal box retrieved several months ago. The photo and the dimensions of the animal container of the outgoing probe were almost identical.

He did not believe this was a coincidence. Wasn't it Sherlock Holmes who said, "When you have eliminated all which is impossible, then whatever remains, however improbable, must be the truth?"

It was then he realized, if he was right, they were about to alter history.... *again*. He tried to call Dr. Chatterling but there was no answer and so he sprinted towards the launching platform of the next probe.

As he ran, he imagined another reality where the time probe had been sent back to the past containing two small test animals, but in this other reality, the test animals selected were two squirrels, the ancient ancestors of the Chi. What would have been the consequences if a modern animal were placed 50 million years in the past and allowed to undergo the normal evolutionary changes as one would expect? What if the design flaw allowed the metal box containing squirrels to break free of the probe and was repeated in the design of the probe about to be sent? If two squirrels had been the source of evolution for the Chi, what would happen if the same event occurred and two guinea pigs were freed into the past? What would be the outcome of the new altered timeline?

Dr. Peck was out of breath when he reached the lab. "Don't send the probe!" he almost shouted at Dr. Chatterling.

Dr. Chatterling startled, then looked up from the computer panel frowning at the concern in Dr. Peck's voice.

"What's wrong?"

Dr. Peck rushed to explain his concerns and his theory. In another alternate reality, they had sent two squirrels back into the past but somehow they had become free and had populated the world and evolved into the species, which was now known as the Chi.

Dr. Chatterling followed the logic of Dr. Peck, although he was disturbed by the idea his species development had been caused by a scientific error of the humans.

"Well, it's too late. The probe has already been sent and it should return any minute," he replied, his voice cold.

The flicker of light, the whine of the collapsing time bubble indicated the probe had returned. The bio technicians opened the cylinder, containing the probe. The computer screen confirmed Dr. Peck's worst fears. The metal container, which had held the test subjects, the guinea pigs, was gone. The defect in the latching system that originally caused the alternate reality, had been duplicated once again. The animal container had broken loose and freed two guinea pigs to a world 50 million years in the past. Dr. Chatterling and Dr. Peck stared at each other in horror as the implications became clear.

* * * * *

DR. CHATTERLING WAS STARING INTENTLY AT THE COMPUTER screen. He was taller than most of his species, standing almost four feet tall. His skin was the color of bronze and he had reddish-brown tufted hair on his cheeks and at the tops of his ears. He kept the hair on his cheeks trimmed so it gave the impression of an old time mutton chop sideburns. His eyes were large, dark and luminous, much larger than the Sissle he worked with. He wore a long coat as was customary to keep his large bushy tail from interfering with his work.

The Sissle were small and stocky with multi-colored patches of skin. They had a short broad face with small ears and generally had very subdued and unassuming personalities. In the past, they aligned themselves with the Chi during the Great Conflict which was the name given to the thousand year war between the Chi and the humans resulting in the domination of the human species. Humans were now only tolerated and served in menial and service positions.

Peck walked to Dr. Chatterling and peered intently into a television monitor on which a large silver cylinder could be seen.

Dr. Chatterling was agitated by the janitor's intrusion at this critical juncture which would forever change the way time and space were considered. The Chi and Sissle had long been working with the recently discovered faster than light particles. It was these particles that led to the breakthrough, allowing them to attempt sending a probe back in time, 50 million years in the past.

"You can empty the trash some other time," he snapped at Peck. "Get out of here."

Peck shuffled off to another part of the lab and continued with his janitorial duties. One of his duties was to clean up the lab where they kept the animal test subjects, which were expected to be used in future experiments. The next experimental step would be to send back in time two mammalian creatures as test subjects, male and female to identify if there were side effects to time travel. He paused and looked into the cage at the almost intelligent eyes of the chimpanzee, which was staring back at him.

TRUE BELIEVER

"I CAN'T BELIEVE THE CONVENTION SENT ME HERE. THIS IS just sheer nonsense," said Reverend Preston, who was on the executive committee for the Southern Baptist Convention. His perfectly styled silver-gray hair, which resembled that of a used car salesman, didn't move as he shook his head in disbelief.

"Well, we're all here to deal with the great 'what if'" Rabbi Schneider said in a low calming voice. He was a small man; slightly balding and wearing wire rimmed spectacles, and who tended to hunch forward thus making himself seem even smaller.

"This is all because Brother Consolmano, the Vatican's astronomer, said that he would be happy to baptize any aliens into the Holy Catholic Church. And then, of all blessed things, Pope Francis says the same thing four years later. Why in the world does the Vatican even have its own astronomer anyway?" whined Preston.

"I agree," Imam Mohammed Abdul Sharif replied. "The news that the Vatican has its own astronomer was quite surprising to me as well.

His statement does bring up some interesting theological issues, although quite hypothetical." The Imam wore the traditional Turkish robe with an embroidered Kafi which accentuated his well groomed beard that was heavily sprinkled with gray.

The three religious leaders were among the over 200 participants attending the quickly called meeting of the World Interfaith Alliance Conference.

It was the news of the unidentified object named Oumuamua that was the impetus for this special meeting of the Interfaith Alliance. When NASA broke the news that there was a new unidentified object entering the solar system with an unusual shape, trajectory and was increasing its speed, scientists and non-scientists, alike, started throwing around words like 'alien probe'. The goal of the conference was to discuss of how the world religions should respond to the knowledge or the arrival of extraterrestrial beings.

"I still think we're wasting our time," complained the Reverend.

"And yet," said the Rabbi, "no one wants to imagine a reality where an entire new species might belong to the Catholic Church and possibly be subject to a solitary man. One can only imagine what technology could be bestowed upon the group that finds favor in the eyes of the newcomers."

The Imam rubbed his temples as if in deep thought or pain, then moved to stroke his beard. "How will we decide what information about the world religions should be presented to alien visitors and which of the world religions should be included? At last count, there are over 4,300 clearly identified different religions. Do we consider the Samaritans who have less than a thousand members in the same light as 2 billion Christians or over 1 billion Muslims? I can't even fathom how we would begin to decide which religions we should teach our alien visitors about."

"That's assuming they even have an interest in religion. For all we know, they might be some type of cyborg race that worships the all mighty and sacred Mother Board," answered the Reverend.

"I agree," replied Rabbi Schneider. "We're being asked to perform the seemingly impossible task of deciding on protocols for a fair introduction of the world's religions to a new species or race but in such a way that it does not favor any one specific religion over another. Frankly, I don't see how it can be done."

There was a chime over the intercom systems signaling the end of the sessions' break.

"Well, I guess it is time to get back to our impossible task," said Imam Sharif. "I pray that Allah gives us the wisdom to discern his will in this matter."

They all nodded in agreement as they returned to the conference.

* * *

MEANWHILE, OUT PAST JUPITER ON THE FLAGSHIP BEZIN'S Blade, Thu'lan looked at the data scrolling across his screen. He made a facial gesture which revealed long rows of razor sharp teeth.

"Reverent Mother, we will be dropping into real space soon behind the large gas planet. The latest probes confirm there are primitive sentient life forms on the third planet."

The Reverent Mother nodded to her first Consort, Tallont.

"The Reverent Mother acknowledges," replied Tallont.

Adorned in jeweled robes, the Reverent Mother sat at the helm of the flagship Bezin's Blade.

"Soon we will be bringing the just law of Bezin to a new world. Praise be, to the new followers who will be joining us on Bezin's way."

Her consort replied, "I wonder how many millions will have to die on this planet before they accept the will of Bezin?" He tried to keep his tone respectful to mask the true depth of his question.

The Reverent Mother shot him a seething look. "Be careful, Tallont. Your heritage as a member of the priest cast will only allow you so much tolerance. You're verging on heresy."

"I beg forgiveness, Reverent Mother." He bowed his head in mock supplication.

"Accepted. Now, let's begin the process of bringing the word of our God Bezin to this heathen planet. As it is written in the Holy Scriptures, 'Let him who hears the word kneel in supplication or feel the blade of Bezin upon their necks.'"

OCCAM'S RAZOR

SPECIAL AGENT DAVID HOWARD WAS A 25 YEAR VETERAN with the FBI and currently assigned to the Washington DC office. As he sat in the waiting room of the secretary of the US Department of Treasury, he absentmindedly rubbed some scars on his hands that he had obtained as an adolescent.

David's father had died by the hands of a drunk driver when David was ten years old, and as a teenager, he worked two part-time jobs to help support the family. One night, as he was walking home from his gig at the local burger joint, he heard terrified screams. He ran to a house which he found engulfed in flames, the sound of screaming children coming from inside. Despite the danger, David ran inside the house and found two toddlers hiding behind the couch. Without hesitation, he grabbed the toddlers and carried them outside. He then went back into the burning house to try to find the mother, but by that time it was too late. The fire department came and dragged him from the house, then transported him to the hospital to take of the burns on his hands.

He was touted as a hero, but he did not feel that way. Local and national news outlets picked up on the story, and Life magazine took a picture of him in the hospital, with his hands wrapped, receiving the Honor Medal from the Boy Scouts, a metal given for scouts who risked their own life in the effort to save another.

When David found out that the two children were left as orphans, he reached out using his media platform to ask that a fund be set up to help support them. He was amazed at how much money was raised by this simple act. A week after he returned from the hospital, he received a phone call from the bank asking for him and his mother to meet with the banking personnel. At the meeting, he found out that other people had heard about his heroism and that he was unable to work for the time being because of his burns. Anonymous donors had set up a fund to help support him and his mother. From that point on, David and his mother always had enough money. It seemed that anonymous donors were continually refreshing the support fund.

When he was a senior in high school, he was called in to the counselor's office and was notified that one of the anonymous benefactors was guaranteeing his college education. His heart was set on George Washington University's criminal justice program, which now was a possibility due to the generosity of his unknown benefactor. The scars on his hands reminded him of the worst day of his life, but also the beginning events that seemed to cement his future.

Still rubbing the scars on his hand, he wondered why he had been called to an emergency meeting with Michael Clapper. Since he was the head of the US Department of Treasury and David himself had an extensive history of working on cases which involved counterfeit, piracy and forgery, he assumed his experience might be the reason for the meeting.

As he set in a plush leather chair in the secretary's anteroom, agent Howard noticed the rich mahogany paneling, which was the height of style in the 1960s. It all seemed dated and yet very elegant. The receptionist was a middle-aged woman staring intently at her computer screen. After a few moments, she looked up and said, "Agent Howard, you may go in now."

Agent Howard entered the room and saw Secretary Clapper and two people he did not recognize sitting at a roundtable.

"Agent Howard, thank you so much for joining us on such a short notice. Please have a seat."

"Thank you," he said as he sat down.

"Agent Howard, this is Glenn Henry, the director of the Bureau of Engraving and Printing, and this is Donna Ortega the director of the United States Mint.

On the table in front of him was an unwrapped package. He noticed the paper seemed very old and discolored. There was also a photo, yellowed with age, and what he recognized as a mint proof set of coins and an uncut page of four of twenty dollar bills.

He now felt sure his original hunch about the meeting being called to discuss an issue of forgery or counterfeiting was correct. He waited until Secretary Clapper spoke.

"A few days ago, a courier delivered this package from St. Patrick's Catholic Church a few blocks away."

Agent Howard raised an eyebrow but said nothing. Through the years, he found it very helpful not to jump to conclusions until he had seen and processed all pertinent evidence.

"I'd like you to look at this proof set of coins and the uncut sheet and tell me if you see anything unusual."

Agent Howard reached across the table to pick up the set of five coins encased in the traditional plastic holder. He was familiar with these mint proof sets of coins as he'd purchased a set of them every year for his two nephews. They weren't really his nephews but that's what they call each other. Fifteen years earlier, his partner had been killed in a raid on a forgery operation that went sour. The last thing his partner asked him to do was to take care of his boys and since that time he'd done everything he could to support the sons of his fallen partner.

"Are you trying to tell me these are counterfeit?"

"That is yet to be determined, but look at them closely," Secretary Clapper said.

Agent Howard once again looked at the proof set of coins. His eyebrows furrowed as he noticed the dates on all of the coins were 2024, four years in the future.

"Is this some type of early release or mockup of coins to be minted in the future?"

"No, and that's the problem," Director Ortega answered. "These aren't in production and the master dies won't even be cast until 18 months before the coins go to minting."

"So, you have a very strange case of counterfeit coins," said Agent Howard.

"That is the conundrum. We have examined these coins thoroughly and the composition of copper and silver is exactly as it should be. The mint marks, lettering, and reeded edges are perfect."

"So, was this some type of typo in the production of the dies?" asked Agent Howard.

"Sir, the United States mint does not make typos," replied Director Ortega, her words terse and clipped.

"So, what you have is a very clever and I guess expensive forgery?" asked Agent Howard.

"Hold that thought," Secretary Clapper interjected. "Show him notes."

"This is what we call a four-note uncut series of $20 bills which is popular and often purchased by numismatists," said Director Henry as he slid the uncut notes over to agent Howard for examination.

At the same time, Secretary Clapper opened up a small drawer and placed a portable UV light as well as a magnifying glass on the table.

Agent Howard picked up the serial twenty-dollar notes and went through his mental checklist for identifying counterfeit bills. First, he identified the watermark embedded which depicted a portrait of Andrew Jackson, and then the twenty on the bottom left of the front of the bill which was printed using color-shifting metallic flecks as well as the eagle and shield image printed with an embossed sparkly ink.

Using the magnifying glass, he quickly identified microprinting under the border to the left of Andrew Jackson's portrait which read, "THE UNITED STATES OF AMERICA 20 USA 20 USA" and the microprinting around the first three letters of each line to the left of the Treasury Department seal which repeats "20 USA". Lastly, he used the tools to examine the mylar security thread which ran vertically at the edge of the paper. The strip glowed with the expected green color and had the correct microprinting of "USA TWENTY" along with a US Flag. Instead of stars, he could see the miniature flag had the numeral 20 printed in the appropriate place.

In his mind, he felt confident these were not counterfeit bills, until he looked at the print date, 2023. He sat quietly for a moment processing all the facts, trying to make a cohesive story that made sense, and then said, "I'm not sure how I can explain the bills and the coins." He was slowly formulating an idea which on the surface was too ludicrous even to voice.

Secretary Clapper cleared his throat, "There is more," he said, sliding the yellowed photograph over to Agent Howard for examination. He noticed it was a picture of some type of ceremony which was staged in front of the US Treasury Building. He could identify Secretary Clapper, as well as who he assumed was the Secretary's wife and a child who looked to be about the age of six or seven along with twins which couldn't be older than three. Other than the fact the photograph looked yellow with age, he didn't see anything distinctive about it.

"What am I looking at? You seem to have a very nice family"

Secretary Clapper leaned forward on his forearms and spoke in a slow and deliberate manner. "In the picture, you will see my wife. We have one child who is two years old and she is currently 18 weeks pregnant with twins. The exterior of the treasury building shows renovations which we have just received funding to begin construction."

Agent Howard paused, furrowing his brow. "A clever Photoshop?"

"We also received the negative with the photo and both have been examined by the forensic staff and have been declared to be original and untouched."

Agent Howard put the photo down and sat back in his chair considering the jigsaw of information he'd been presented. His mind went back to one of his instructors at Quantico who taught him about Occam's razor - "If you eliminate the impossible, whatever remains, however improbable, must be the truth."

"So, you think we're dealing with… artifacts from the future?" Agent Howard could hardly believe the words he was saying. It seemed to defy all logic, but then he couldn't think of a more logical explanation. "Where did you say you got these from again?"

"We all understand how hard this is to believe, but the last piece of the puzzle seems to support this theory, even though on the surface it is crazy. As I said, the package came from St. Patrick's Catholic Church. In 1819, St. Patrick's Church was trying to raise funds for a new chapel. They decided to bury a time capsule and, for a $10 donation, a person could put something into the time capsule. Last month it was the 100th anniversary of burying the time capsule and when they opened it, they found this package."

Secretary Clapper showed him the brown wrapping paper which had the words printed on it, "PLEASE DELIVER TO SECRETARY CLAPPER AT THE UNITED STATES TREASURY"

"Our forensics lab has confirmed the paper is in fact 100 years old, but the ink used is from a modern Sharpie marker. Treasury agents have examined the time capsule and where it was buried at the church and they can find no signs of tampering," continued Secretary Clapper.

"If everything I have seen today is true, I think we must consider, no matter how unbelievable, someone or something has the ability to travel through time," said Agent Howard, tapping his fingers on his chin.

"I know it sounds crazy but it's the only conclusion which fits all the parameters of the puzzle and this is why we have called in the FBI. If there is some person or organization that's discovered and developed the ability to travel through time, the national implications are frightening. It makes the risk of nuclear warfare pale by comparison," said Secretary Clapper.

"I would like to take all of these artifacts back to the FBI for our own analysis, and then I will notify you with the results. If our results confirm yours, and you are correct, then some dark Pandora's Box has been opened and the potential consequences threaten the entire world," replied Agent Howard in a very somber tone.

A week later, Agent Howard found himself in a large conference room where there were close to thirty persons representing members of the president's cabinet, all of the national security agencies, representatives of the military, NASA, DARPA as well as the director of the FBI.

The director of the FBI, Gerald Searle, began to speak. "Ladies and gentlemen, you have all been briefed on an ongoing investigation into the possibility of someone or some organization has discovered and perfected time travel. The implications are frightening and far-reaching. At this point, I will turn the meeting over to Agent Howard for further updates."

"Thank you, Director Searle." Howard stood up and walked to a podium where a laptop was set up. "You all have the briefing dossier and I would first like to assure you the evidence has been thoroughly examined by the forensic laboratory here at the FBI and has been confirmed by the labs at DARPA. We have recently received information from two other news sources which seem to have a bearing on this case."

He hit a key on the laptop on the podium and a video began to play on several screens around the room.

On the corner of the video was the National Geographic logo. The narration began.

> We are here at the excavation site of Jefferson's Monticello. Archaeologists are currently excavating a washroom built in 1808 when it replaced the kitchen in the newly built South Wing when the first floor of the South Pavilion was buried with 3 feet of fill dirt to raise the floor's elevation. This is where the slaves did the laundry for Jefferson's family, as well as all other workers and those enslaved on the Monticello property.
>
> It seems archaeologists have found a metal container which has been unseen for over 200 years.

The footage showed a young woman carefully brushing the dirt off of a metal object. As more dirt was being removed, the camera zoomed in for a close-up. The archaeologist is heard to say "What the fuck?" What has been exposed is the top of a Smithsonian lunchbox with the large words 'OUR SOLAR SYSTEM' printed over a picture of the planets.

The video then switched to a scene of a lab where the archaeologists were about to open the lunchbox.

> Here we are at the universities' archaeology lab where they are about to open up this incredible, yet impossible, find. No one can yet explain how a modern-day lunchbox became buried in ground untouched for over 200 years. Speculation

is, this must be some type of clever hoax, although by who, or how, it was perpetrated cannot be explained.

The camera showed several scientists, all wearing white gloves, getting ready to open the lunchbox. The latch is rusted with age but slowly becomes undone under the gentle prying of the archaeologist's hands. The lid is finally raised. The camera zooms in showing the contents of the lunchbox which consists of a sheet of postal stamps measuring five down and seven across. The subject of the stamps is commemorating Martin Luther King Jr.

As the video ends, there was significant murmuring around the room.

"This is just the tip of the iceberg. Here is a photo from an archaeological dig at the Nottingham Castle in England. Along with artifacts dating back to 1742, they found a Hawkeye action figure from the Avengers."

"Here is a Swiss Army knife found during excavating of the Roman City of Sanisera in Spain dating back to 15 BC. Next we have a Chinese checkers game found while the Chinese were doing repairs on some of the earliest sections of the Great Wall of China dating back to 500 BC."

"How many of these artifacts have now been discovered?" one of the DARPA scientists asked.

"To date, there have been twenty-four reported artifacts from the future. We assume there may be many more that were likely thrown away by archaeologists who couldn't believe what they had found and assumed it was trash. That happened in this next case."

Agent Howard once again touched the keyboard and a photo of a dashboard Jesus was displayed. "When this was originally found at the archeological dig in Jerusalem, it was thought to be a joke and tossed into the trash. Later, when reports started coming in from other archaeologists about artifacts from the future, they retrieved this item and found out it was, in fact, over 2000 years old, and yet, an artifact from the future."

Agent Howard once again pushed a key on the keyboard which brought up the picture of the large neck thermos bottle next to a vaginal vibrator. This photo elicited a small ripple of muffled laughter.

"This was found under ten feet of volcanic ash while excavating a brothel in the city of Pompeii, which was destroyed in 79 A.D. The vibrator had been placed in the thermos to protect it from the heat of the volcanic ash. Artifacts like these are now showing up all over the world. Archaeologists originally thought it was some type of clever hoax, and yet all of the artifacts have been confirmed to be the appropriate age for the archaeological dig although they are all from the future. Whoever's doing this seems to have a sense of humor about the artifacts in relation to where they are placed, and at this point, we have found no evidence of malevolence. Although anyone who has this technology has the ability to change history and that, ladies and gentlemen, is why we are gathered here today."

* * *

JOHN THOMPSON II WAS BORED. AS HE SAT IN HIS LUSH leather chair, he absentmindedly stared off into the distance while he was swirling his Hennessy Ellipse Cognac in a crystal St. Louis Thistle Gold brandy sniffer. He lived in the family home his grandfather had built in 1910. Residents of Hartford Connecticut would have considered this to be one of the older mansions of the city, but for him it was just the family home.

One of the unforeseen consequences of unlimited wealth was boredom. When there was no limitation due to money, when you could have everything or do anything you desired, eventually you ran out of things to capture the imagination.

John reflected on the events which brought him to his current state of tedium.

He had been raised in Springfield, Illinois. His father, a single parent, had a thriving garage where John had worked at from an early age. He had an uncanny knack with mechanical devices, and could often could just listen to the sound of a car's engine and diagnose the malfunction. The other mechanics in the garage used to wager on John's diagnostic intuitive gift.

His father died when John was twelve years old, and he was sent to live with his grandfather who was his namesake, in Hartford, Connecticut. His grandfather, John T. Thompson, was the inventor of the Thompson submachine gun. The boy found a home in the machine shop of the Colt Firearms Manufacturing Company. He began to work on the assembly line but quickly demonstrated the ability of design and began working on improvements for the internal mechanisms of the Thompson submachine gun, as well as other firearms.

In 1942, he joined the Army. During boot camp training, he and other recruits were being drilled on the use of the Thompson machine gun. Next to him, the recruit was struggling with his gun jamming. John was in the process of dismantling it to figure out the issue for the recruit when the sergeant walked up.

"Which one of you dumb fucks broke one of the government's finest killing instruments, and what in the hell are you doing trying to take it apart?" growled the sergeant.

"Sergeant, this gun has a broken recoil spring and I was going to fix it," John said as he snapped to attention.

"And just how in the hell would a green piss ant private like you know that?"

"Well, if you listen, you can hear a click at the end of the ejection process." John released the guns bolt action to demonstrate.

The sergeant cocked one eyebrow. "And where did you learned about a Thompson machine gun?"

"From my grandfather, John Thompson. He invented the machine gun. I've been working on them since I was a kid, and I actually designed the trigger release mechanism for this model."

"Well boy, this is your lucky day. I'm sure the brass will have other plans for you when they hear about your experience."

Within a week, John was relocated to a heavily guarded research facility in lower Manhattan where he was working with the team on a new upgrade for the Norden bomb sight. He stayed at the facility, where he advanced to the rank of captain supervising several weapon projects, until the end of the war.

In the summer of 1947, he was ordered to proceed to the town of Roswell, New Mexico. Even though he had top-secret clearance, he was required to sign multiple forms with words like, 'treason under penalty of death', in bold print. Upon his arrival, he was escorted by military police to a jeep where he was driven to a remote area of scrub brush and desert. As they topped a hill, he could see the wreckage of some type of craft. His work on bombsights during the war gave him a thorough and intimate knowledge of American aircraft, but what he saw didn't fit into any known category. There was a large, heavily armed contingency of soldiers on site and he was taken to a group of a dozen men, both military and civilian. The tension among the soldiers was palpable, and he also detected an air of fear. Whatever was going on, was outside of the realm of normal.

The colonel in charge was tall, with a short military haircut, and looked to be right out of central casting for any Hollywood war movie.

"Gentlemen, my name is Col. Hastings. Before we go any further, it is my duty to remind you that what you're about to see is of a top-secret nature. If you share any of this information outside of approved channels, you will be breaking the National Securities Act and will be subject to prosecution with the most severe punishments available under the law. You have been chosen for your expertise in your respective fields, and it will be your mission to reverse engineer this aircraft."

One of the civilian scientists raised a hand. "How do you know it is an aircraft?"

The Colonel glared at the man indicating his displeasure at being interrupted. "There were four pilots retrieved from the wreckage who are being examined by a medical team. After you have had a chance to examine the craft in its original state, it will be taken to a secure base where you will have the ability to thoroughly analyze every component. I cannot emphasize enough the high level of security you will be under. We assume this technology is not from any known government and if the reverse engineering succeeds, our military readiness will leapfrog decades ahead of our enemies."

There was murmuring among the group as the words of the colonel and their meaning became clear.

As the group of scientists and engineers walked through the crash site, the strong smell of ozone assaulted their noses. They were confronted with torn and twisted metal wreckage and mechanical items which they could only guess at their purpose. After their cursory examination, John was placed on a bus and taken to Edwards Air Force Base where he was placed in a barracks separate from the rest of the base's contingency of soldiers.

* * *

OVER THE NEXT SEVERAL MONTHS, THE GROUP KNOWN AS the Dirty Dozen, began itemizing and categorizing each mysterious and exotic item. The name, Dirty Dozen, came from the term used to identify the twelve watch companies who made pristine waterproof watches for the military. During this process, John found a small box with writing in a language he'd never seen, with several dials and switches. Something about the simplicity of the box intrigued him. Loose wiring indicated it had been connected to some type of energy source at one time.

Late one evening, John was alone in the lab and was applying current in slow, deliberate increments to the unknown device when a screen on the box glowed with life. Four sets of alien symbols appeared. He experimented with turning one of the dials and saw the symbols changed. Through trial and error, he deduced the symbols were sequential numbers. He returned the numbers to their baseline status. There was a switch on the box which he intuitively thought resembled an off/on switch.

On a note pad he noted the time on the wall clock was 0200 hours. He dialed in a single alien digit and, wondering if he was about to blow himself up, he flipped the switch.

Nothing happened... or so he thought.

He looked at the clock and was surprised when he saw the time read 0155. He glanced at his watch which showed the time to be 0212. Confused, he flipped the switch off. To his amazement, the wall clock time changed to 0212.

He spent the next hour or so contemplating what had happened and its ramifications. Another test was in order. There was Victor Bakelite AM radio in the lab. He tuned it into KOMA out of Oklahoma City, which was the only station on at this time. The time was 0330 and Frank Sinatra was singing *Someone to Watch Over Me.*

He flipped the switch again and once again, the time went back 15 minutes and another song was on the radio. After a 15 minute wait, the wall clock showed 0330 and to his amazement, the same Sinatra song came on. The switch was turned off and the clock returned to the normal time.

There could be no mistake. The device was able to move time backwards. He had discovered an alien time machine. The discovery excited him as well as filled him with terror. The ability to alter the time line was too great a power for any government to possess. He destroyed his notes, hid the device behind a filing cabinet and went home to plan his next steps.

A week later, he put his plan into action which involved getting the device into the garbage, followed by a late night ninja visit to the base's dump. Once the device was in his possession, he waited another week to make sure no one was suspicious, and then drove to Hartford where he hid the alien device in his basement. After another month of waiting, there was no evidence his superiors had any idea of his treasonous activities. He made excuses relating to his health and turned in his resignation and waited for the paperwork to go through. Then he returned to his home and began his study of the device in earnest.

It took several years of trial and error until he understood how the device worked. The dials controlled the parameters of minutes, hours, days and years. The limiting factor was power, as the further one traveled back in time, the more energy was required. His first need was unlimited wealth, which was easy to obtain by going back in time and investing in the stock market. Dow Chemical, GE, IBM, etc. bought at their inception provided a mass fortune.

Since the limiting factor was energy, he put billions into the research and development of the battery. He funded R&D into the development of the first practical zinc-carbon battery. This led to the development of the lithium-ion battery and eventually the graphene battery which store significant amounts energy. With each development in energy storage, he was able to travel farther back in time and allowed modifications of the time machine to become mobile. The entire machine was engineered to fit into a backpack and weighed a mere twelve pounds. The next issue was deciding what to do with a time machine. Traveling back in time was straight forward, but travel to the future was more complicated. Since the future has so many potential outcomes, travel to the future was limited to only 3-4 years.

John understood the tremendous risk of making a small change in the past. Even something seemingly minor could result extreme and unexpected historical effects. He had read the Ray Bradbury short story *Sound of Thunder* where the future was changed by the simple act of stepping on a butterfly 66 million years in the past. He knew any rift in the timeline could affect his own future, or possibly his very existence.

So, he pondered about what to do with this most fascinating and dangerous device.

He found when he traveled to the and past; the time machine would cast a time field bubble approximately ten feet in diameter in which he could interact with the local area. Also, as long as he was within the bubble, he was invisible to anyone outside of the time field. All they would see would be light distortion similar to a heat haze seen in a mirage.

His big idea was to set history right through the use of historical time traveling.

Years later, he had seen it all… literally.

He knew how the pyramids were built.

How Cleopatra looked.

What happened to Malaysian Airlines flight MH370.

Who Jack the Ripper was.

He knew the truth about Amelia Earhart, the Mary Celeste, the lost colony of Roanoke, King Arthur, Atlantis, the assassination of Kennedy and Oak Island. He knew it all.

All that he had learned, he put into a book, *The Truth of History*.

He understood the book would be seen as science fiction or historical heresy. He needed proof, which led to the idea of the great prank.

At any one time, there were hundreds of archaeological digs in progress worldwide. His first proof of concept time trip was to Thomas Jefferson's plantation, Monticello. He traveled to Virginia with Martin Luther King commemorative stamps and a Smithsonian lunchbox. It was quite easy to get to the site of the archaeological dig, set the time coordinates for 1808, travel back in time, bury the lunchbox, and then return to his own time.

After the success in Virginia, he started traveling around the world to plant ancient Easter eggs to be discovered in 2020.

∗ ∗ ∗

JOHN THOMPSON HAD JUST CELEBRATED HIS 96TH BIRTHDAY and he realized he was reaching the end of his own life. Only a few more breadcrumbs to place before his grand scheme would come to fruition. Slowly sipped brandy warmed him, and a smile came to his face.

* * *

AGENT HOWARD WAS WORKING IN HIS OFFICE WHEN HE received an excited phone call from the research lab asking him to come immediately. They'd found something. Reaching the lab, he discovered a group of technicians gathered around a computer terminal. Mark Russell, the lead researcher, quickly waved for Howard to come to the computer terminal.

"Boss, I think we got lucky. We were examining the Swiss Army knife found in Spain, and when we opened up all of the blades, we found a partial print. We traced it back through all known databases and found a match to a John Thompson who was working on top-secret military armaments at the end of World War II. He then was selected to work on another top-secret program but most of that information has been redacted. There are references to Area 51 and the Roswell crash site in New Mexico."

"You mean the crash site of the supposedly alien craft?

"Yes sir, that is correct."

Agent Howard did some quick math and said, "Is he still alive? He must be close to 100 years old. What do we know about him?"

Mark looked at his notes. "John Thompson II is a multi-billionaire living in Hartford, Connecticut. His grandfather was the inventor of the Thompson machine gun and left his grandson a significant inheritance. Then through a number of very lucrative stock deals, he amassed a fortune but he stayed out of the public light. As a result, we know very little of his personal life. We were very lucky he made this mistake."

Howard frowned. "Whoever is behind this doesn't seem like the type to make a sloppy mistake. It doesn't add up. If this is the person who has the ability to travel through time, then whatever we do has already happened, so therefore it must be part of his plan. We need to go visit him, but we must be careful because on some level, this may be some sort of a trap. Although, for what purpose, I have no idea."

When he arrived back at his office, Howard found a certified letter had been delivered by courier. He opened it to find a short note:

Agent Howard, please come alone. John Thompson II

A cold chill swept over Agent Howard, as if he had just stepped into a winter storm. How do you approach someone who possibly knows the future events that are going to happen?

There were several meetings to discuss the next steps, which ranged from a full armed response to a simple one-on-one meeting. Since no crime had actually been committed, there was no justification for an armed assault on Mr. Thompson's Hartford home. It was decided agent Howard would go alone, but there would be a significant military presence nearby in case the need arose. He would be wired for video and sound, and have a GPS chip placed in the heel of his shoe.

As Howard drove up to the estate's gate, he noticed there were multiple cameras and other electronic surveillance devices. He started to push the intercom button when a voice said, "Welcome Agent Howard. Please proceed to the main house." The gate opened. Howard became aware of a complex mixture of fear, apprehension and excitement. A servant met him on the porch and led him to a large and elegant study. Sitting in a plush leather chair, sipping brandy was a very elderly man who he assumed was John Thompson. Beside the chair was a green oxygen tank with tubing leading to nasal prongs which John was wearing.

"Agent Howard, please excuse me if I do not get up. Please have a chair. Would you like something to drink?"

"No, I am fine," he said as he took a seat.

"Good. Then instead of me answering 1,000 questions, let me just tell you a story, starting at the beginning."

He started with his involvement in World War II weapons design, being selected for the Roswell investigation, the discovery of the alien time device, his historical time traveling, and ending with the 'time pranks'.

"That is one hell of a story. I think I would like that drink after all," said Agent Howard as he tried to wrap his mind around all he had heard over the past 60 minutes.

As a butler arrived with a brandy for Agent Howard, John said, "I wish I could've been at those meetings when you were discussing the Easter eggs I had planted through time," he said with a mischievous twinkle in his eye. "I would have loved to see the expressions on everybody's faces. I hope you enjoyed my quirky sense of humor."

"In all honesty, we were more focused on the national security implications of your time pranks."

"I can assure you that, at this time, there are no national security implications which should concern you. I have gone to great lengths to ensure there would be no changes to the past which would have implications today."

Howard paused for a moment, sipping his brandy. "You can understand the governments concerned about this technology and how it could be misused."

"I very much agree with you, which is why the technology will be destroyed after one last trip. Time travel is too much of a temptation for those who feel they are wise enough to know how to best change the future." John reached for a backpack which was sitting next to his chair. "Agent Howard would you mind standing next to my chair?"

Cautiously, Howard put his glass down and walked over to John, who slipped a hand inside the backpack. There was a flicker of light and then they were both on a muddy road in what looked to be colonial Connecticut.

"What the hell?" Howard exclaimed.

"Sorry for the dramatics, but I thought an actual demonstration would be the quickest way of proving of the story I told you. The year is 1635, and what you are observing is when Governor John Haynes brought over 100 English settlers to Hartford to open up trade and commerce with England."

The FBI agent was speechless as he watched settlers in traditional clothing of the 1600s. There were wagons being pulled by oxen along a muddy road, buildings of roughly hewn wood, and several pack animals loaded down with animal furs.

"We can't leave the time bubble, but it's all fascinating, isn't it?" With that, John flipped some unseen switch inside the backpack and they returned to his study. "If you want, you can save some of the mud on your shoes for carbon dating, should you need further proof this was not some type of elaborate hoax or hallucination."

Howard looked down to the mud on the shoes, then walked back over to his chair and picked up his brandy, resisting the urge to consume more than a sip at a time. His mind was having difficulty processing everything he'd learned over the past hour. The proof of aliens, time travel… it was almost too much to absorb.

"So what's the purpose of all of this? What is the endgame?"

"There is no endgame." Then with great effort, John picked up the backpack and walked over to a wall which had a small metal door. He opened up the door, placed the backpack inside, and then hit a button. There was a slight vibration and a sound of rushing wind. John walked back to his seat. "Well, that's it. It's over."

"What you mean, 'it is over'?" Howard asked nervously.

"The device has been vaporized in a fusion furnace, so there can be no reverse engineering or malevolent use."

"What?" he exclaimed. "You just destroyed, what is possibly, the greatest discovery of all mankind?

"Of course," John said in a very matter-of-fact way. "Do you know any government or private agency you would trust with this technology knowing all the damage that could be unleashed on the world?"

The agent fell silent, for he knew John was right. This type of technology was too dangerously powerful to be trusted in anyone's hands.

Howard felt as if a heavy weight was pushing him into his chair. He felt drained and numb as his mind was processing all of the numerous implications of what had just happened.

"What's next?" he asked hesitantly.

"I'm sure it is obvious to you, I'm not in good health. My doctors have only given me a few months to live. So, I decided to go out with a bang. On the table next to your chair, you will find a book I wrote journaling my story, as well as the answers to many historical mysteries."

Howard looked at the book on the side table entitled *The Truth of History*. He picked it up and scanned the table of contents which covered everything from the extinction of the dinosaurs to the source of the Covid-19 pandemic. Inside the cover of the book was a flash drive and a signed acknowledgment to agent Howard.

"So this is it? This is everything?

"Well, yes and no. Everything that's happened since you drove up to my gate until the time we returned from 1635 has been recorded. The video was then transmitted to over 20 processing centers throughout the world where it was added to the flash drive of over 1 million copies of my book. As we are speaking, over 100,000 couriers are delivering copies of this book to all respectable historians, government leaders, heads of state, and leaders of industry. It is also being posted on websites throughout the world. My goal was to make sure this information was not suppressed or claimed to be a hoax. This has been my life's work I wanted to make sure it saw the light of day."

The agent rubbed his temple as he felt the beginnings of a headache. "You know, you just let the genie out of the bottle."

"That is true. My only hope is the alien technology is so far advanced it will take hundreds of years for it to be reproduced. Hopefully, by that time, man will have reached a level of maturity that will allow him to responsibly use this incredible gift."

After their meeting, a small army of agents descended upon the home searching for any diagrams or notes relating to the time machine. The house was clean, showing no evidence of the fantastical story.

Six weeks later, John Thompson II died and was laid to rest in the family cemetery.

As the information in John's book became public knowledge, there was much debate about the book being a hoax, or a government cover-up. Too many people in the government and the scientific community knew the truth for the story to be buried.

Several months later, after the initial explosion of news and internet speculation had died down; Howard was in his Washington office when he was notified that there were two men asking to speak with him. When they identified themselves as attorneys for the estate of John Thompson II, he took the meeting.

They explained that according to John's will, a majority of his billions was left to multiple charities. They handed him an envelope which was simply inscribed with his name. He opened it up and read a letter from the late John Thompson.

Dear David,

I hope you don't mind the informality, but after all that we have been through, calling you 'Agent Howard' seemed rather inappropriate. I saw your story in Life magazine from your childhood years ago, and I've been following your life since that time. You may have guessed that I was your Guardian Angel who helped support you and your mother, as well as your educational needs. I have thoroughly vetted you and watched how you have always been there for your deceased partner's family. You are a good and decent man. Therefore, I'm leaving you my home in Connecticut as well as the sum of $1 billion to do with as you wish. I have no doubts that you will use this windfall to do good things.

It was a great delight to meet you. I hope on some level, that you enjoyed my warped sense of humor. I wish we could have known each other longer, but to quote Chaucer, "time and tide wait for no man".

Peace,
John Thompson II

P.S. I took a small peek into the future and when you meet a young lady named Catherine Marie, take her someplace nice for lunch.

ODE TO THE HUNT

I HAD THE STALKING BEAST IN MY SIGHTS. IN ONE SECOND HE would be dead. I had hunted all the large beasts of Earth, the giant swamp rats of Hargere's Outpost and the three-horned whiptail on Cererus. Out of respect and love of the hunt I still used my antique Merkel Custom .470 which fired lead projectiles fueled by a solid explosive charge.

But then the beast turned and looked at me with large golden flecked eyes and his gaze seemed to penetrate into my soul and I had the thought that I was looking into his soul as well.

And as we stood there, in the warmth of binary suns, with the sweet scent of the lemon thistle gently floating over the purple hazed plains, there passed between us an understanding that we were both brothers on this planet Theisilon 5.

We shared the same air, the same warmth of the suns, the same passions, and the same life force.

I smiled with the knowledge I had just discovered, a sacred truth, a grand secret of life.

I lowered my gun and the stalling beast, also smiling and moving with unbelievable speed, calmly ripped out my throat.